MW01615706

W~~h~~

about ~~R.J. Patterson~~

"R.J. Patterson does a fantastic job at keeping you engaged and interested. I look forward to more from this talented author."

- Aaron Patterson
bestselling author of SWEET DREAMS

DEAD SHOT

"Small town life in southern Idaho might seem quaint and idyllic to some. But when local newspaper reporter Cal Murphy begins to uncover a series of strange deaths that are linked to a sticky spider web of deception, the lid on the peaceful town is blown wide open. Told with all the energy and bravado of an old pro, first-timer R.J. Patterson hits one out of the park his first time at bat with *Dead Shot*. It's that good."

- Vincent Zandri
bestselling author of THE REMAINS

"You can tell R.J. knows what it's like to live in the newspaper world, but with *Dead Shot*, he's proven that he also can write one heck of a murder mystery."

- Josh Katzowitz
NFL writer for CBSSports.com
& author of Sid Gillman: Father of the Passing Game

"Patterson has a mean streak about a mile wide and puts his two main characters through quite a horrible ride, which makes for good reading."

- Richard D., reader

DEAD LINE

"This book kept me on the edge of my seat the whole time. I didn't really want to put it down. R.J. Patterson has hooked me. I'll be back for more."

- Bob Behler
3-time Idaho broadcaster of the year
and play-by-play voice for Boise State football

"Like a John Grisham novel, from the very start I was pulled right into the story and couldn't put the book down. It was as if I personally knew and cared about what happened to each of the main characters. Every chapter ended with so much excitement and suspense I had to continue to read until I learned how it ended, even though it kept me up until 3:00 A.M.

- *Ray F.*, reader

DEAD IN THE WATER

"In Dead in the Water, R.J. Patterson accurately captures the action-packed saga of a what could be a real-life college football scandal. The sordid details will leave readers flipping through the pages as fast as a hurry-up offense."

- Mark Schlabach,
ESPN college sports columnist and
co-author of *Called to Coach*
and *Heisman: The Man Behind the Trophy*

THE WARREN OMISSIONS

"What can be more fascinating than a super high concept novel that reopens the conspiracy behind the JFK assassination while the threat of a global world war rests in the balance? With his new novel, *The Warren Omissions*, former journalist turned bestselling author R.J. Patterson proves he just might be the next worthy successor to Vince Flynn."

- *Vincent Zandri*
bestselling author of THE REMAINS

OTHER TITLES BY
R.J. PATTERSON

Cal Murphy Thrillers
Dead Shot
Dead Line
Better off Dead
Dead in the Water
Dead Man's Curve
Dead and Gone
Dead Wrong
Dead Man's Land
Dead Drop
Dead to Rights
Dead End

James Flynn Thrillers
The Warren Omissions
Imminent Threat
The Cooper Affair
Seeds of War

Brady Hawk Thrillers
First Strike
Deep Cover
Point of Impact
Full Blast
Target Zero
Fury
State of Play
Siege
Seek and Destroy
Into the Shadows
Hard Target

TARGET ZERO

A Brady Hawk novel

R.J. PATTERSON

For Ed, one of the best men I've ever known

CHAPTER 0

Berbera, Somalia

HAWK FIGURED HE HAD five minutes to live, ten if he was lucky. The rope binding his hands behind his back burned as he slowly twisted his wrists in an effort to break free. The scent of sweat and grease wafted from the gag secured around his head. In front of him, an armed man paced back and forth, eventually shedding his shirt to combat the sweltering heat. Hawk couldn't wait to remove his own shirt, but first things first: he needed to escape.

Sweat poured down Hawk's face, stinging his eyes. But the pain wasn't enough to distract him from the task in front of him. Small but deliberate movements had already started to loosen the rope's constriction on his hands. Hawk stared at the survival knife dangling from the guard's belt.

If I can just get my hands on that knife . . .

Hawk noticed at least two sets of feet that flashed by periodically beneath the only door leading into the room. A small elevated window was the only other potential exit point. Hawk thought it would be a tight fit but that he'd still be able to squeeze through the opening to the other side. What was beyond that window, however, was merely a guess.

Hawk had only been conscious for fifteen minutes and awoke in his current position. The armed guard still pacing around the room had ignored all of Hawk's questions so far. The only time he'd heard the man speak was when another man entered the room and said everything was going to happen in about twenty minutes and to be prepared.

The overhead fan spun slowly, failing to create much of a breeze. It creaked as it turned. Hawk eyed it cautiously, not because he was annoyed with the noise but because he surmised it could serve another purpose.

Hawk initiated his plan, which started with a gargling noise to get the guard's attention. The guard marched over to Hawk and glared.

"What do you want?"

Hawk threw his head back and forced out some sound. It was unintelligible in any language, partly by design, partly due to the gag shoved into his mouth.

The guard leaned closer to Hawk. "What did you say?"

Seizing the opportunity, Hawk threw his head back before unleashing a vicious headbutt on the guard, who staggered backward. Hawk rose to his feet, bringing the chair with him. The guard let out a yelp, an obvious effort to attract the other guards' attention. But the men stationed outside the door never heard him.

Hawk placed one of the legs on top of the man's throat and sat down. The man struggled to get free, putting his hands on the chair and hurling it upward. Seconds later, the chair hit the ground, shattering and breaking Hawk loose.

The guard opened his mouth to alert his fellow guards about what was really happening behind the door. But his cry for help was thwarted again, this time when Hawk punched the man in the face.

"Where is she?" Hawk demanded.

The guard furrowed his brow and pulled back. "Where's who?" he said, coughing as he spoke.

"Where's the woman? You know who I'm talking about."

"I don't know. Across the street, perhaps."

"I'm not going to ask again."

Quivering, the guard relented. "She's being held across the street."

Hawk then delivered a vicious blow to the man's throat, shattering his trachea. As the man collapsed to the ground, he writhed on the floor in an attempt to breathe. Any suspense that he might regain his breath and alert his fellow guards that he needed their help vanished when Hawk wrapped the remains of his bindings around the man's neck.

The man fought hard, putting both hands on the rope and tugging at it. But he couldn't prevent Hawk from choking the life right out of him. In less than a minute, the man stopped fighting and slumped to the ground, dead.

Hawk ripped a knife from the man's belt and positioned the only other chair in the room a few feet away from the overhead fan. He backed up and took a running start, reaching a swift speed before stepping up onto the chair and leaping for the fan. Hawk grabbed the fan and spun around once. He then grabbed a steel support beam that hung a couple of feet above the fan and shimmied toward the small opening. Swinging his feet back and forth to gain momentum, Hawk lunged once, breaking the window.

Hawk cleared the glass around the edges of the frame with his foot and slipped through the hole he'd created. He climbed down to the outside, landing in an alleyway between two unfamiliar buildings.

He was free, but he wasn't leaving until he got what he'd come for.

CHAPTER 1

Six months earlier
The Ajagar
Arabian Sea

ARAV KATARI SURVEYED THE DECK of his ship and smiled with satisfaction. If he had his druthers, he would've been standing over the deck of the *INS Vikramaditya*, India's premier aircraft carrier. But he was content with his plight in life, even if every family member tried to convince him otherwise. Running a cargo ship between India and various Middle Eastern and East African ports was enough to satiate his childhood dream of spending his days at sea. But this day at sea was different.

The dark clouds forming to the south didn't bode well for the remainder of his journey, but that wasn't what concerned Katari the most. Pacing around the deck, he couldn't help but take his eyes of *the* container. Officially, it wasn't even onboard, purposefully omitted from the ship's manifesto. If a storm caused the ship to capsize or some other calamity struck, no one would know the contents of container No. 8942. Yet it was exactly how Katari's supervisor wanted it.

Katari didn't want to ask what was inside the container, but he felt duty bound if for anything the safety of his crew. His first request as to the contents was stonewalled, but he persisted.

"What if something happens and it begins to leak, spread, or waft over the deck?" Katari pleaded. "I need to know how to keep everyone away from danger."

"Fine," his supervisor said as surveyed the deck. "It's methylphosphonyl difluoride. Are you happy now?"

Katari had never heard of the chemical compound; he wasn't sure he wanted to either. When he finally researched it, he discovered it was used to make sarin gas.

"You're putting a chemical weapon on my boat?" Katari said when he confronted his supervisor.

"Technically, that's my boat. And it's not a weapon yet. Just do as you're told. Your job depends on it."

Katari exited his supervisor's office in a huff. While Katari would've preferred to quit his job in that moment, he couldn't. His wife and three young children wouldn't have appreciated such a commitment to principles when it came time to buy food at the local market or pay their rent. His aging parents—who lived with him and his family—wouldn't appreciate it either. And neither would his brother, who still hadn't found a job.

When the containers were loaded onto *The Ajagar*, Katari filled out the manifest as instructed. Container No. 8942 was omitted from any official report. However, Katari was told not to worry about it because it wouldn't matter. Whatever was inside wouldn't arrive in port, making Katari's protests moot.

"What do you mean?" Katari asked his supervisor.

"You'll understand when it happens," he replied.

As Katari surveyed the deck of *The Ajagar*, he still wondered what his supervisor had meant by that comment. They'd been at sea for over seventy-two hours and were nearing the Berbera port in Somalia when he first noticed the pair of ships speeding toward them across the horizon. Once the boats pulled up portside to *The Ajagar*, Katari knew exactly what his boss meant.

Several armed men boarded Katari's ship and began to search different containers. When they came to No. 8942, one of the men pulled out a pair of deadbolt cutters and clipped the lock. The doors swung open to reveal a dozen barrels. The pirates began loading the fifty-five gallon drums onto their boats and managed to be surprisingly efficient. In less than half an hour, they were gone.

Talman Virk, Katari's second in command, didn't even wait until the pirates had disappeared on the horizon before he suggested they fill out an incident report. Katari protested, insisting that it wasn't necessary. Virk rejected Katari's protests and proceeded to quote large swaths from the employee guidebook. At first, Katari ignored Virk. But then Katari realized Virk was not only serious, but he felt the need to act immediately.

After the incident, Katari was alone on the bridge when Virk entered with a clipboard in hand.

"Captain, I'm having a difficult time finding container No. 8942 on the manifest. Can you help me locate it?" Virk asked.

Katari sighed and shook his head. "I already told you that you don't need to fill out an incident report. I'll handle it."

"No, you said we don't need to fill one out at all," Virk said. "So, I thought I'd take care of it for you."

"And again, I insist that you give it a rest."

"Give it a rest? Give it a rest? Captain, those men stormed aboard our vessel and stole some of our cargo. It's unacceptable. We must report this."

"It might be unacceptable and, yes, we're obligated to report it—but not right now. I'll take care of it. That's part of my duties as captain of this ship."

Virk furrowed his brow. "Perhaps, but it's also my duty to assist you when you're too busy. And you appear to be in dispose right now, so I'm simply offering my services."

"And I'm declining them."

Virk cast a suspicious eye toward Katari. "Very well. But before I go, will you please explain to me why container No. 8942 was left off the manifest?"

"It's not important."

"Not important? That's against the law, not to mention our own shipping company's protocol."

"Drop it," said Katari as he narrowed his eyes.

Virk sighed and sat down, insistent upon filling out the incident report.

"I'm warning you," Katari said.

Virk held up his index finger. "Noted. Now, leave me alone so I can finish this report."

"You can't finish the report," Katari said, brandishing his knife. "It's time to put down the report and your pen and exit the bridge."

"Says who?"

"Says me."

Katari snatched the form from Virk's hands and ripped it up.

"How dare you," Virk snapped.

"I'm not going to ask you again to leave the bridge."

Virk stared at Katari's knife. "You have no idea what you've done. I'm going to report you. You'll lose your captain's position. Maybe they'll even give it to me."

Katari didn't hesitate, lunging at Virk. Virk dodged to the left and then to the right several times before Katari plunged his knife into Virk's midsection.

Virk doubled over and slunk to the floor. He looked up at Katari with a face pleading for answers.

"Why? Why did you do this?"

"I warned you to drop it, but you wouldn't listen."

Katari grabbed the microphone and made an announcement that was broadcast throughout the ship, requesting that all crew members meet in the galley for an emergency meeting.

Virk held his stomach, which was bleeding profusely. His hands were now soaked in blood as he tried to stop the flow. Unfortunately for Virk, his efforts were to no avail.

"It's time for you to go," Katari said.

With a face pleading for answers, Virk looked up at Katari. "How could you?"

"I could ask you the same question," Katari said.

Katari opened the door to the bridge and led Virk down the steps before giving him a forceful nudge over the side and into the water. As he watched Virk splash into the sea, Katari struggled to believe what he'd just done. He watched as Virk flailed, crying out for help. In a matter of seconds, Virk was little more than a meek cry for help.

Katari leaned on the railing of the deck as he stared out across the water. He despised what he'd become, but he had no choice. Virk had forced Katari's hand.

Katari took a deep breath and exhaled before turning and heading toward the galley. He needed to address the crew about the pirate incident.

He also needed to tell them about Virk's suicide.

CHAPTER 2

HAWK PULLED BACK A CHAIR from the table and waited for Alex to have a seat. The dinner patio at The Riad la Tangerina was worthy of a postcard, something Hawk had little doubt was already available in the hotel's gift shop. Yet he had his eye on the woman sitting across the table from him for two reasons: her beauty and her mystery.

While they waited for J.D. Blunt to arrive, Hawk ordered a bottle of wine and admired the view.

"Hard to believe that's all that separates Africa from Europe," he said, gesturing to the water.

"The Strait of Gibraltar isn't much of a barrier these days," Alex said. "I think you and I both know that firsthand."

Hawk nodded. "Yes, but do you realize that my

21

firsthand knowledge about you is very minimal. I mean, you know all about me after digging through my past, but I hardly know your past."

"What's there to know? I blew the whistle on some CIA project and got kicked to the curb. And here I am."

Hawk shrugged. "So you say."

Alex eyed Hawk and looked pensive for a moment before responding. "Are you being coy right now? I hope so, because the way you're acting is starting to make me feel like you're being combative."

"All I'm saying is that I'd like to know a little bit more about who you are and your past, that's all. I don't play games. You should know that about me by now."

The waiter slipped up to the table and uncorked a bottle of wine before filling both their glasses and scurrying away.

Alex relaxed her shoulders and took a gulp of her wine. When she finished, she turned her gaze toward the water.

"It's because there are some things that aren't so easy to talk about, the kind of memories you wish you could bury and never unearth again."

"I think I have a lifetime of those already, but I don't let it stop me from sharing it with others. Shouldering the burden of such pain alone is never healthy."

Alex sighed. "I'm not sure I agree with that. Reliving

a painful past seems to trigger depression for me."

"Maybe you've never talked about it with someone who understands you."

"You think you understand me?"

Hawk nodded. "I'm getting there. Try me."

"Fine. What do you want to know?"

"You know the crazy story about my parents or at least who I thought was my parents. But I never hear you talk about yours. What are they like?"

Alex grabbed her glass of wine and drained it before answering. "It's because they're dead."

Hawk leaned forward and placed his hands on top Alex's. "I'm so sorry, Alex. I didn't know."

Alex's lips quivered, her eyes watering. "It's okay. It's just that I hardly got to know them. They died when I was eight, though it wasn't much of a life. Dad was an analyst for the CIA; mom was a double agent working for Russia. I think they only stayed married because it was smart for their careers."

"And you?"

"I'm sure I was a mistake. No one working in intelligence who has aspirations of climbing the ladder wants to be burdened with children."

"What happened to them?"

"Car accident on the beltway. The crash was so fiery that they cremated the bodies. Had to finish the job, I guess."

"And you just accepted that?"

"I was eight years old. What else was I going to do? Demand to see dental records and compare them? But if either of them survived, I'm sure they would've contacted me by now."

Hawk nodded knowingly.

Before the conversation continued, the waiter approached the table, carrying a platter with a plain white envelope on top.

"Mr. Hawk," the waiter said, offering the letter. "This is for you."

Hawk took the letter and thanked the waiter, who hustled away from the table. As Hawk carefully opened the letter, he stopped and looked at Alex.

"What do you think this is all about?" he asked.

She shrugged. "Love letter from an admirer?"

"Let's hope not," he said with a wink. He turned the card over and read it aloud.

Mr. Blunt requests your presence in a private room off the main dining area.

Alex furrowed her brow. "I don't know about this. Wasn't he specific on wanting to meet us out here on the veranda?"

"That's what his text said."

"Why the change of venue? It doesn't make sense."

Hawk picked up his glass of wine and stood. "Let's go find out what's going on."

CHAPTER 3

J.D. BLUNT CLIPPED THE END of his cigar before he jammed it into his mouth. The sweet tobacco taste from the Nat Sherman 1930 Coronado Grande settled over his tongue. He took a long pull on his glass of scotch and glanced at his companion across the table before directing his gaze toward the doorway.

"You seem a little on edge," the man said.

"For good reason," Blunt said. "I'm anxious to get this over with. The fact that three key figures from Firestorm are going to be in the same room at the same time doesn't make me feel at ease."

"We can always cancel if—"

"No, let's just keep it brief, all right?"

The man nodded.

A few moments later, the door opened and Hawk and Alex strode into the room.

"Senator," Hawk said, offering his hand.

Blunt shook Hawk's hand and then Alex's. Remaining standing, Blunt gestured toward the other man.

"Hawk and Alex, I'd like for you to meet Senator Christopher Roland, a trusted friend of mine for over two decades and an ally for Firestorm."

They all exchanged pleasantries before taking their seats around the small round table.

"Why the change in meeting place?" Hawk asked.

"You can never be too careful," Blunt said. "My friend here has already noted just how nervous I've been about this meeting."

"Let's get it over with then," Alex said.

"Yes, what's the meaning of all this?" Hawk asked.

"Senator Roland?" Blunt said.

"Thank you, J.D.," Roland said as he turned his attention to Hawk and Alex. "As you might be aware, Al Hasib is getting more aggressive and more brazen in their efforts to obtain powerful weapons. Their latest attempts include an effort to acquire a chemical weapon."

"And they've never been able to do this before?" Hawk asked.

"Not yet, though Al Hasib has inquired about it with different arms dealers in the past."

"What's different about this time?" Alex asked.

Roland took a deep breath then exhaled. "This time, they're probably going to get it unless we stop them—pardon me, unless *you* stop them."

"What's the mission?" Hawk asked.

"Hassan Garaar is a small-time weapons dealer in northeast Somalia," Roland began. "Intel reports say that he's gained enough methylphosphonyl difluoride to weaponize sarin gas."

"How much gas are we talking about?" Alex asked.

"We're not sure about how much yield he'd be able to produce from the shipment he received, but it'll be enough to kill several thousand, maybe more, in the right setting in a large metropolitan area."

"And how do you intend for us to stop this deal?" Hawk asked.

"In person, of course, at the docks in Berbera, Somalia. Garaar is tentatively scheduled to make an exchange with an operative from Al Hasib on Saturday night. We need you there to seize control of the weapon."

"Are you out of your mind?" Alex asked. "We need more help than this."

"Technically, you are the help," Roland said. "We've got a guy on the ground in Berbera already."

"Then why even use us at all?" Hawk asked.

"This guy can't do it by himself, and we can't risk

bringing in even a small contingent of forces to Somalia. Since the 90s, everything action we've taken there has had to be handled discreetly. I'm sure you understand."

"I get it," Hawk said. "I don't want my body dragged through the streets if anything goes wrong."

"Exactly. You two did so well stopping the threat in Washington that I thought you'd be perfect for this task. And quite frankly, since time is of the essence, I don't have anyone else I can turn to."

"We're your last hope?" Alex asked as she leaned forward.

"You may be the last hope for thousands of unsuspecting Americans, too," Roland said. "I feel far better about stopping this threat before it has time to take shape than trying to eliminate it while some Al Hasib agent runs around New York City with enough sarin gas to wipe out a crowd at Yankee Stadium."

"You in, Alex?" Hawk asked. "You know I need you on this."

She let out a long breath. "I'm in on one condition. I need to know who we'll be working with."

Roland nodded. "Fair enough. He's a former special ops guy who worked for the CIA. You might have worked with him before, Alex. His name is John McGinn."

Alex leaned back in her chair and interlocked her

fingers behind her head. "McGinn? That's your guy on the ground?"

"What do you know about him, Alex?" Hawk asked.

"He's an interesting character," Alex responded. "I find it hard to believe that the CIA would place him in a place like Somalia. What's he doing there?"

"Nothing of too much consequence," Roland said. "Just training some Somalian military personnel."

Hawk watched Alex look up and bite her lip. He didn't flinch, hoping she'd agree to go.

"I don't like being on location, but I'll do it," she said.

"Excellent," Roland said before standing up and handing her a pair of folders. "Everything you'll need to know for the mission is in there. Good luck."

CHAPTER 4

HASSAN GARAAR TIGHTENED HIS MASK and carefully opened the fifty-five-gallon drum in front of him. He slid a small tube into the barrel and siphoned out some of the liquid. He placed a few drops onto a petri dish to examine the liquid.

Still good.

He closed the drum and used a dolly to move the container to another part of his warehouse. Returning to his work area, he stooped down to get eye level with the caged brown-and-white hamster treading on a wheel. He watched the small animal run tirelessly for half a minute.

Better run while you still can, Barbara.

Garaar never named the animals he tested his product on—almost. But he knew the hamster was going to die a gruesome death. As a result, he decided to name the hamster after a woman he dated at Caltech. Garaar caught Barbara cheating on him with a lab partner and employed restraint at the time.

You just keep right on doing what you're doing, Barb.

Garaar adjusted his mask again and hovered over the device that would weaponize the sarin and make it far more potent. Every inch of the vaporizer was checked before he closed the small kit and latched it shut. He locked the main entrance to warehouse before carefully loading the case into his vehicle and climbing into the driver's seat.

"See you soon, Barb," he said before shoving his SUV into drive and kicking up enough sand to constitute a dust storm in certain parts of California.

While Garaar drove, he considered the path that led him to this moment, the point that he considered to be a crowning achievement in his fledgling career. The fact that he could mix his own sarin gas was reason enough for celebration. It was, after all, the primary purpose for his educational exploits in the United States. However, he was far from achieving his end game, which was to create massive quantities for Al-Shabaab. But his superiors needed a way to generate some funding for their next offensive after the U.S. and Europe conspired to freeze the organization's bank accounts. Ultimately, Garaar knew Al Shabaab didn't have the vehicle to deploy a weapon like this in an effective way. Yet, he didn't complain, content to ply his trade until that moment arrived.

In his dream scenario, Garaar would've preferred to remain in Saudi Arabia and train for jihad in a much grittier way. At one time, pulling the trigger on a sniper rifle aimed at American soldiers seemed to be a much higher calling. But he came to understand his role in eradicating the infidels from the face of the planet, a role that was less barbaric in practice but far more barbaric when it came to results. At least, it appeared that way to him when he watched videos of what happened to test subjects when exposed to sarin gas.

The live test was the final hurdle he needed to clear in order to take his weapon to market. He'd already lined up a buyer and established a date for the sale. However, he realized that no one would pay the kind of money he was demanding for a chemical weapon unless it was proven to work. Garaar was also anxious to see for himself if he indeed implemented everything he learned while earning his chemical engineering degree. At this stage, failure would be disastrous and quite possibly could cost him his life. He needed to ensure the batch of sarin he mixed was every bit as potent as it could be.

Selecting a test subject wasn't particularly difficult. He spoke with a doctor working in conjunction with the World Health Organization who told him about a small village thirty miles northwest of Berbera that had a viral outbreak of polio. Authorities placed the village under quarantine while epidemiologists attempted to isolate the source of the outbreak. In the meantime, the only people allowed in or out of the village were health personnel.

Garaar glanced down at the WHO credential hanging around his neck. The credential belonged to an Indian doctor Garaar had stabbed to death earlier in the week. He wasn't proud of murdering the man, though technically he was still an infidel and deserved such a fate. When it came to Islam, all other religions stood at odds with it, even Buddhism. But it was tame compared to what he was about to do.

He flashed his credentials to the armed guards patrolling all the roads leading into the village. They waved him through. Garaar checked his notes and turned left at the first intersection and drove a quarter of a mile until he reached the designated home. He worked quickly to assemble his camera and carry it into the house along with the weapon. If any snoopy neighbors appeared, his cover would be blown, resulting in an even larger-scale test. For now, all he wanted to do was get a record to verify the effectiveness of the gas and escape the village without further incident.

The woman who greeted Garaar at the door begged him to hurry.

"My children need you," she said. "Come, quick."

Garaar followed her into the main room of the house where two small children were lying down. He estimated the older girl to be four and the younger one to be about age two. The four year old wallowed in a pool of vomit while the two year old cried incessantly.

Putting on his mask, he directed the mother to the other side of the room next to her children. He turned on the camera and set it on the tripod. Then, without warning, he unleashed the gas.

In less than a minute, the mother and her children were dead. And Garaar was pleased that it worked as quickly as it did. He wasn't sure he could take much more of the gurgling and gagging noises the trio made as they died. He proceeded to store all his equipment before drenching the inside of the house with gasoline. He unfurled a 100-foot rope, soaked it in gasoline, lit the rope on fire, and drove away.

Garaar passed through the checkpoint and was at least a mile outside the village before he saw large plumes of smoke billowing in his rearview mirror. He picked up his phone and dialed a number.

"I completed the testing," he said. "The product will be ready for you to collect on schedule."

He couldn't wait to demonstrate the gas on Barbara.

CHAPTER 5

Berera, Somalia

HAWK SLUNG HIS BAG over his back and descended the steps of Blunt's private jet. He stopped at the bottom and stared at the runway that stretched for as far as he could see. Heat haze emanated from the tarmac. Looking down at his feet, Hawk watched two beads of sweat splash to the ground.

"Welcome to Somalia," a man said in a thick accent.

Hawk looked up to see a man smiling and offering his hand. Shaking the man's hand, Hawk flashed a smile back before he strode toward the private hangar.

"What kind of airport is this?" Alex asked.

Hawk looked over his shoulder to see Alex's mouth agape as she stared down the runway.

"What on earth needs a landing strip this long?" she asked, still in disbelief.

Hawk stopped. "Nothing on earth, but something landing on it does."

"Come again?" she said as she gathered her equipment bag and hustled next to him.

Hawk resumed his walk toward the hangar. "This runway was a backup emergency landing site for the U.S. space shuttle program during the 80s. Cost the government $40 million a year just to have the privilege of renting it in case of emergency."

"If only I'd decided to pave a three-mile stretch in the desert."

The man who'd greeted Hawk slipped up beside him and tried to take his bag.

"Let me help you with this," the man said.

Hawk tightened his grip on the straps. "Cool your jets, my friend. I can handle it myself."

"Very well then," the man said. "Right this way."

The man gestured toward an SUV sitting near the entrance of the hangar.

"My name is Cawaale or you can just call me 'Lucky,'" he said.

"Lucky? Now how'd you get that name?" Alex asked.

"My mother was eight months pregnant with me when our village was overrun by a group of pirates. They killed everyone except my mother, who pretended to be dead."

"That's quite a story, Lucky," Hawk said as he watched Lucky lumber toward the vehicle with a pronounced limp. "What happened to your leg?"

"I was attacked by a crocodile."

"That's not so lucky."

"I'm still here, aren't I?"

"Touché."

Hawk opened the door for Alex and then climbed in after her. Cawaale gave them a brief tour, covering a vast expanse of Berera history, from the flourishing ivory trade in the ninth century to the Russian military presence in the 1970s.

"If tourism ever becomes a thing in Berera, you need to switch jobs, Lucky," Hawk said.

Lucky flashed a 100-watt smile at Hawk and whipped around the corner before skidding to a stop.

"We're here," Lucky said as he jammed the gear into park.

Hawk and Alex got out and walked up to a gated compound. The cinder block walls towered twelve feet above, providing a formidable barrier to the outside and casting long shadows to escape the scorching heat. The sounds of men shouting and yelling were mixed with scuffling and fighting. And Hawk assumed it was all coming from inside the compound.

Hawk pressed a button next to the door and waited. A few moments later, a voice crackled over the intercom.

"Please state your name and business," a man said.

"I'm Brady Hawk, and I'm here with my assistant Alex. We're supposed to be meeting with a John McGinn."

"Just a moment please."

Thirty seconds later, the gate swung open, revealing a hive of activity that was every bit and more than what Hawk imagined. Two men shuffled back and forth, battling with a pair of wooden sticks. One man hurled a grappling hook over a wall that appeared to be used for training. Two other men sparred in hand-to-hand combat simulation. Meanwhile, dust swirled about the area and almost choked Hawk. He coughed several times before he looked up to see the man he'd been waiting to see.

"You must be Brady Hawk," the man said, offering his hand. "John McGinn."

Hawk nodded. "Pleased to meet you."

"And you must be Alex."

Alex smiled and nodded before shaking McGinn's hand.

From his shirt pocket, McGinn pulled out a new pack of cigarettes and tapped it hard against the palm of his hand. He proceeded to rip the package open, tossing the cellophane wrapping onto the ground. He fished out a cigarette and placed it loosely on his lips.

Before he lit up, McGinn offered Hawk and Alex a smoke.

Alex waved him off; Hawk scowled.

"I'll pass," Hawk said. "Those things will kill you."

McGinn flicked his lighter and took a long drag. He gestured with his hand around him then exhaled a lung full of smoke.

"This is Somalia, Mr. Hawk. Lung cancer won't kill you here. You'll never live long enough for it to catch up with you."

"We don't intend on staying long," Alex said.

"Get ready because we're going till the world stops turning while we burn it to the ground tonight," McGinn said as he took another long drag. "Follow me. You're going to need to get situated in our state-of-the-art secure facility."

Alex leaned close to Hawk and whispered, "Did he just quote Nickelback?"

"God help us," Hawk said under his breath.

They followed McGinn as he navigated through the men engaged in combat training.

"Don't pay them any attention," McGinn said. "They couldn't hurt a flea."

"Aren't you the one supposed to be training them?" Alex asked.

"Lady, you sure do ask a lot of questions. I'd

suggest you keep your mouth shut. A woman talking too much is far more detrimental to her own health than smoking ever will be. You can take that to the bank."

"Any other nuggets of wisdom for me?" she said, chiding him.

McGinn ignored her dig. "No matter what you do, don't ever anger the camels."

Hawk glanced at Alex, who rolled her eyes.

"This guy's a piece of work," she said quietly.

"That's one way of putting it. It's far nicer than I would have," Hawk whispered. "I might just have to punch his lights out before we're through here."

McGinn entered a set of barracks and marched through the hallway until he came to an open door.

"This will be your room for the next several days. Feel free to smoke in here if you like."

Hawk furrowed his brow. "What? No private room for the lady?"

McGinn shrugged. "It's the 21st Century. Get over it."

Hawk, who'd grown more annoyed by McGinn's antics by the second, rammed his forearm into McGinn's chest and pinned him against the wall.

"I think she'd like some privacy," Hawk said. "You think you can make that happen?"

McGinn exhaled and cut his eyes skyward. "You

Millennials are so damn high maintenance, I swear."

Hawk released him. "We aren't anything other than highly-trained operatives who are here to bail your ass out. I suggest you quit acting put out or we'll go get on a plane and leave you to stealing one of the most lethal gases in the world on your own."

McGinn put up both hands in an act of surrender. "Now, now. No need to be so offended. I was just making an observation."

"Observations are usually intelligent," Alex quipped.

McGinn shook his head. "Follow me, Alex. I'm sure I can find you a room down this hall somewhere."

Hawk stopped at the room next to his. He pushed the door open, revealing an unoccupied space. "This one will do."

McGinn forced a smile and cocked his head to one side. "This one it is. Room No. 12 for the lady."

Alex pushed her way past McGinn and threw her bag on the bed.

McGinn tugged on his ratty New England Patriots hat. "So, you and Hawk aren't a thing?"

Hawk chuckled as he took in the scene. Alex slammed the door in McGinn's face.

"Are you always this hospitable?" Hawk asked.

McGinn blew a lung full of smoke upward. "Hospitality isn't really my thing. Busting people's balls is."

Hawk shook his head and looked at the grimy floor. "So, when are we going to put together a plan?"

"You just leave that to me."

Alex opened the door, rejoining the conversation. "We didn't come here to be your puppets."

"You settled in awfully quick," McGinn said. "Don't you want to put your bag up? Just leave the men alone, and we'll take care of all the logistics. You just do as you're told. Understand?"

Alex sneered at him. But before she could say a word, the building was sprayed with bullets. Glass shattered in the rooms and spilled into the hallway. Instinctively, the trio dropped low to the ground and moved away from the doorway.

"You got any idea who this is?" Hawk asked as he checked the magazine in his gun.

McGinn shrugged. "I've got plenty of enemies."

"The kind of enemies who can infiltrate your state-of-the-art secure facility?" Alex chided.

"Just keep your head down if you want to get out of here alive," McGinn said. "This isn't the first time we've been attacked here."

"Not much loyalty among your men, is there?" Hawk said.

"This isn't the time for your critique," McGinn said as he stood up. "Now, get ready to follow me."

McGinn didn't get a chance to take a step before another round of bullets rained down on the building. He dropped back to the floor.

"Got any other ways out of here?" Hawk asked.

CHAPTER 6

Washington, D.C.

EMILY THORNTON SETTLED into a chair in the stark conference room. Silhouetted figures carrying boxes and other large objects passed along the opaque windows surrounding her. The floor was cold and bare. Nothing about the room was inviting, though she was certain that was the point. The business of Searchlight wasn't about creating a warm environment; it was about snuffing out any and all threats. And Emily wasn't sure if Searchlight had finally concluded that Brady Hawk was the kind of threat that needed to be dealt with using extreme measures. She only hoped it hadn't arrived at that decision.

The door swung open, and Kade Parker strode in. He sat down directly across the table from Emily.

"What do you think of the new place?" Parker asked, gesturing around the room.

"You need an interior decorator," she said.

"That's not exactly where we like to spend our resources, though we wouldn't have had to get a new facility if the old one hadn't been compromised under your watch."

"That doesn't change the fact that this room is still ugly."

"I'll mention that to HR," he said.

"Searchlight has an HR department? Who knew?"

Parker leaned back in his chair and exhaled a long breath. "Look, the reason we're here is to discuss where we're at with Hawk and Alex. I trust you have some more information about them."

"If you're expecting any bombshells, I'm afraid you're going to be disappointed," Emily said. "They spoiled the bomb threat at Nationals Park, and Hawk, at least, has become a cult hero on the Internet. A few security cameras captured him, although the images are grainy. His identity is likely secure, but he's being called *The Real Chuck Norris*. There was even a hashtag with that same name trending nationally on Twitter last week."

"I don't care what the public thinks about Hawk; I want to know what you think about him in terms of his threat to this organization."

"Searchlight isn't exactly his primary concern

right now. However, kidnapping his little girlfriend probably put you on his radar."

"I guess the only real question I want answered today is this: Do you think we'll still be able to use them?"

Emily took a deep breath, her gaze cutting back and forth around the room as she thought. She needed to give the right answer to Parker, one that wouldn't raise any suspicion.

"It's possible," she finally said.

"If you're not one hundred percent sure, we need to eliminate them," Parker snapped.

"Trying to gauge that right now is a big challenge. I'm not sure I'd be comfortable with—"

"You've got a week to make your definitive conclusion," Parker said before he stood up. "One week, and then I want your final answer."

She nodded.

"Do you know where they are?" he asked.

"They're in Somalia now."

"Good. I'll put Thor on alert and have him ready on standby."

"How am I supposed to make that determination from here?" she asked.

"Better book a flight for Somalia."

CHAPTER 7

Berbera, Somalia

RASHID QURESHI RELOADED and peered through his binoculars across the compound for any more traitors. The Al Hasib operative engaged in a quid pro quo with Al-Shabaab. When Al Hasib entered into negotiations to secure a chemical weapon from Al-Shabaab's top chemical engineer, the proposed exchange involved more than just money. Al-Shabaab was losing the battle when it came to recruits due to the CIA's covert training facility in Berbera. The CIA had built a compound to help Somali military develop a special ops program to combat the guerilla tactics of Al-Shabaab. And after watching dozens of potential recruits flock to the CIA-sponsored program, Al-Shabaab leadership decided to eliminate it.

Qureshi had worked for weeks to prepare

Al-Shabaab forces for a surprise attack on the compound. And so far, everything had gone as planned with one small exception: Inexplicably, only a little over two dozen of the more than two hundred recruits were present when Qureshi began the attack. While dead bodies littered the training grounds, Qureshi hoped for a much better result.

We must have a spy.

Qureshi scanned the area once more through his binoculars and noted at least one figure standing in the doorway of the barracks. He gave the order to fire again, unleashing another round of munitions at the building. Then everything fell silent.

Qureshi reloaded again when the voice of Pendar, Qureshi's tech expert, pleaded with Qureshi to look at his phone.

"I sent you some screenshots off the security feed," Pendar said. "It appears as though there are some important guests visiting the compound this week."

Qureshi unlocked his phone and called up the pictures Pendar had sent. Qureshi squinted at the image before enlarging it.

"Is that who I think it is?" Qureshi asked.

"If you think it's Brady Hawk, then yes."

Qureshi broke into a wide grin.

Allah must love me. I will avenge my brother's murder.

Qureshi needed to tell Al Hasib chief Karif Fazil about the new developments taking place in their raid on the secret CIA training camp. Qureshi dialed Fazil's number.

"Is everything all right?" Fazil asked.

"It's better than all right," Qureshi said. "This might be a far more productive trip than you ever imagined."

"How so?"

"We have all but secured the compound as we speak. However, there are some surprising guests paying a visit to the facility this week who might be of interest to you."

"And who would that be?"

"Brady Hawk and Alex Duncan."

Fazil laughed. "Never question that Allah is on our side."

"I thought the same thing."

"I don't care about the girl, but make sure you capture Hawk alive and bring him back to me."

Qureshi hung up.

I'll try, but I'm not going to make any promises.

CHAPTER 8

HAWK CRAWLED ON HIS STOMACH back to his room and grabbed another gun and a couple clips out of his pack, which he threw over hs shoulder. He made his way back into the hallway and glanced at McGinn and Alex. The shooting had stopped, and they hadn't heard much noise other than a few commands shouted intermittently.

"I need to see what's going on out there," Hawk said.

McGinn grabbed Hawk's arm and pulled it down. "Don't even think about it."

Hawk shook his arm free of McGinn's grip. "I'm not asking for your permission."

"Don't move," McGinn said. "We need each other to stay alive. We don't need your cowboy bullshit right now."

"If you knew how to actually secure a compound, maybe I wouldn't have to take a chance," Hawk said as he started to stand up.

McGinn yanked Hawk's arm down again. "What's your problem? You're going to get us all killed."

Hawk slunk to the ground and clicked his safety on.

"Thank you," McGinn said. "Now, we're safe for the moment, but don't think I haven't planned for this moment."

"What kind of moment are you talking about? The kind where one of your trusted men betrays you?" Alex asked.

"That's exactly the moment," McGinn said. "Rule number one of working in East Africa is simple: trust no one. It's also rules two through ten. So, yeah, I don't even trust you two yet, but I'll take my chances since you've only hit me while those guys out there are shooting bullets at me."

"You have a way to get us to safety?" Hawk asked.

McGinn nodded. "Follow me."

He got up, remaining hunched over and low to the ground. Alex and Hawk followed the man's lead. They all hustled down the hallway and took a sharp left into a cozy office about ten meters before they reached the far end of the building. McGinn locked the door behind them and went to work.

He slid a shelving unit to the side, revealing a

small panel in the wall. Opening the panel, McGinn revealed a passageway out of the barracks. He gingerly placed his foot into the hole.

"Gotta test the ladder first," McGinn said, answering a question that neither Hawk nor Alex had yet vocalized. "I think it's good."

"Hawk, you want to have the honors?" McGinn asked. "You secure the area down there. Then Alex, then me. I'll cover our tracks in case they search the room."

Within ten minutes, they were all safely in the underground passage. McGinn removed the ladder and led them to a secure room beneath the home of an elderly woman a quarter mile away from the compound.

"We can get in and out of this room through a small opening in a cellar we dug for her," McGinn said.

"How did you arrange all this?" Hawk asked.

"We pay her a monthly stipend. Not enough to change her standard of living to the outside world, but let's just say she eats very well."

"So, now what?" Alex asked.

"We still need to secure the passageway in case any of those Al-Shabaab thugs figure out where we went and try to come after us," McGinn said. "Hawk, I'll need your help."

"What about me?" Alex asked.

"Just stay here. We won't be long."

Hawk glanced at Alex, who cast a leery eye toward McGinn.

"Here, take a gun," McGinn said, handing it to Alex. "You'll be safe here, and if you need to get out, the opening to the cellar is in the bathroom."

Hawk watched Alex, who appeared to be fine with McGinn's solution.

"Let's go," McGinn said.

Hawk followed McGinn into the tunnel.

***

ALEX CHECKED THE CLIP and counted the bullets. She felt foolish for not doing this in McGinn's presence as he could've easily handed her an empty gun or a clip with only a couple bullets. Not that she would need more than one shot to shoot him. No matter how cool and in charge McGinn tried to be, she didn't trust him.

With nothing else to do, Alex decided to snoop around. If she had time, she would open up her computer and start snooping around on the Internet, breaking into classified servers and digging up information on McGinn. Instead, she decided to pry the old-fashioned way.

She went straight to McGinn's desk in the corner of the room. Taking a moment to remember where everything was positioned, she then began to dig through the papers in the drawers. At first, it all seemed like boring administrative paperwork. But then she came across one file that arrested her attention. She started reading, and her mouth went slack-jawed.

Unlocking her phone, she took several pictures of the papers before returning everything to how it was when she first entered the room. She then read more of the documents by looking at the images on her phone.

Hawk is never going to believe this.

CHAPTER 9

Wednesday

HASSAN GARAAR STRUGGLED to shake the scene from his mind—the mother gasping for air as she watched her children die. It was not the side of the cause he wanted to witness again. Garaar desired to put his talents to use for jihad as best as possible. He was certain when he started that it never would've consisted of betraying the trust of a sick family and locking them in a room with vaporized sarin.

Anything for the cause, right?

The end justified the means, but it didn't make Garaar feel like he could stake a claim on the high road of this conflict now. The American military may have killed his family and other friends, but he knew he could no longer look at himself in the mirror and claim to be better. No amount of nuance or mental gymnastics could help Garaar talk himself out of his new reality: He was a murderer.

If that realization wasn't enough to sober up Garaar, paranoia set in on the chemist. Ever since he returned to his warehouse to prepare the sarin and vaporizer for sale, he couldn't shake the feeling that he was being watched. Garaar wasn't one to dismiss the feeling without a thorough investigation. It's why the night before he had covered the windows with sheets and reviewed every square meter of his office in order to make sure he could speak freely. While he found nothing, it didn't stop him from installing a sound machine in his office to protect against any audio snooping. It also didn't stop him from moving the sarin to his home and in a protected wall safe located in his bedroom closet.

Garaar used his phone to call his Al Hasib contact.

"Do you have someone down here already?" Garaar asked.

"Why would you even ask me that?"

Garaar looked around, peeling back the curtains to peek outside. "Just answer the question."

"Absolutely not. We have limited resources as it stands, and we haven't sent anyone to your location."

"Are you sure?"

"Have you been drinking?"

Garaar slammed the phone down, irked at how evasive the responses were.

Five minutes later, Garaar's home security system alerted him to intruders at his residence. He rushed home only to discover the aftermath of a whirlwind search. Couches were flipped over with cushions strewn about the room. Garaar also found every drawer had been dumped onto the floor and apparently sifted through in search of something. He suspected whoever initiated the search was looking for the sarin.

Garaar rushed to his closet and opened the wall safe. The sarin was still there. In an impulsive move, Garaar decided to return the sarin to the warehouse and hide it there. The security was sufficient enough, and the perimeter had never been penetrated, even though he'd previously felt more vulnerable there than at his home. His sense of security at his house was apparently overinflated, and nothing could reassure him now.

Surely they don't know what I'm doing.

He glanced at the barrel in the corner that contained his personal stash of sarin. Despite being compensated for his services, Garaar figured he couldn't live off the meager stipend supplied by Al-Shabaar. Not comfortably, anyway. He held back a small portion that he intended to sell privately to the highest bidder. No one would ever know.

Though he was starting to question that

assumption given the recent break-in and paranoia he was experiencing. Perhaps someone did know.

But the lure of the big payday trumped his fears.

Garaar looked around his lab and continued with his work for the day, confident that everything would be fine as long as he could make it until Saturday night without anything else going haywire.

CHAPTER 10

ALEX SLEPT WITH HER PHONE, almost never setting it down when McGinn was around. She wanted to tell Hawk about what she'd found, but it was difficult when McGinn acted as if Hawk had to shadow him wherever they went. She presumed it was because McGinn was a fraud who couldn't fight his way through a room full of kindergarteners. That was her first impression of him, at least. Perhaps he was a fully competent operative. But she'd have to see him in action to change her mind.

She was left behind again while Hawk and McGinn returned to the compound to see if it was still occupied by the men who'd attacked or if they'd found what they were looking for. Either way, she was told it required a high degree of caution and she could best serve them by going over schematics he printed out for her.

Alex hovered over the blueprints and tried to

figure out the best place for them to tap into the security network so she could have eyes on the building throughout the duration of the operation. The execution of what she was being asked to do was simple to her, so simple that it made her question why she was even tapped for the job. When she initially asked why not anyone else, Roland's reasoning made sense, but now she began to suspect there was something else going on. Her task was something dozens of tech experts could do in their sleep.

And if McGinn is such a badass, why does even need Hawk?

In her short time with Firestorm, if she'd learned anything, it was that she needed to be on her guard at all times and trust no one. And she took her own advice to heart with the exception of Hawk, who'd proven himself to be more than trustworthy. She still held Blunt suspect, even though she wasn't quite sure why.

A couple hours later, Hawk returned with McGinn and updated Alex on everything that transpired at the compound. The power had been cut off along with the water. More than two dozen men had been killed, their bodies left in the center of the courtyard, while the ones who escaped had yet to return to the grounds. McGinn explained that he and Hawk donned disguises and sought out one of the men who'd been training at McGinn's camp. The trainee, Amir, described what happened after they left.

According to Amir, the militia that initiated the attack were looking for something, but they didn't appear to find it. Amir watched the scene unfold from a crack in the door at one of the storage sheds. The soldiers kicked the door down, but not before Amir had time to hide behind some supplies in the corner. After a cursory search, the soldiers abandoned the room and moved along. Fifteen minutes later, they were gone, screaming and cursing in anger.

"Should we abandon this op and come up with another plan?" Alex asked. "Sounds like there are some things that are getting beyond our control here."

McGinn glared at her. "Everything's fine. According to my sources, the exchange is still on. This attack had everything to do with Al-Shabaab's vendetta against the presence of a U.S.-led training facility here and was merely coincidental."

Hawk nodded. "And you trust this informant?"

"I'd bet my life on it," McGinn said. "In fact, I *am* betting my life on the information he gave me."

"In that case, we should still proceed," Hawk said. "What's at stake here if this weapon gets into the wrong hands is worth the risk."

"Not if we're dead," Alex said. "Who's even going to find out what happened to the weapon if this is a set up?"

Hawk put his hand on Alex's shoulder. "We still need to try to do what we came here to do."

McGinn cracked his knuckles. "That's right, Alex. Listen to your partner. I'm in charge here, and there's no reason to doubt my informant. I can promise you that the exchange is going to happen as planned."

"That's why I'm concerned," she said.

McGinn eyed her closely. "Come again?"

"This information all feels like it's coming too easily to me, as if someone is feeding it to you for other purposes."

"Are you suggesting my informant is screwing with me?"

She shrugged. "Not sure. But I'd be leery about taking anybody at their word."

McGinn smirked and looked at Hawk. "You might wanna tell your girl here that paranoia will get you killed in this business."

Hawk narrowed his eyes. "One person's paranoia is another person's savvy intuition. Alex reads situations well. I'm trusting you, but if she's insistent that something else might be at play here, I think we'd be wise to use more caution."

"And how do you think we should do that?" McGinn asked.

"Get someone else to confirm it. Get Alex to hack someone's communications. Anything to get us the assurance we need that we're not all being set up here."

McGinn exhaled slowly. "You sure did change your tune fast. A little defensive of your princess, aren't you?"

Hawk grabbed McGinn by his shirt and got in his face. "You got something against Alex?"

McGinn huffed through his nose. "You gonna do something about it if I do?"

Hawk released McGinn before shoving him backward. "Get your act together or we're out of here."

"Be careful about your demands, Mr. Hawk," McGinn said as he smoothed out the front of his jacket. "There's no private plane sitting on the runway for you, and getting out of Somalia on the ground isn't a picnic. I suggest you get in step with my plan and do what you were sent here to do, which is help me keep that weapon out of the hands of terrorists. Are we clear here?"

"Get the confirmation or we walk."

McGinn sighed and shook his head. "I'll do it later, but right now we need to get moving and scout out the location of the exchange. We still have to finalize our plans for Saturday night."

CHAPTER 11

EMILY THORNTON WATCHED as Hawk and Alex piled into an SUV with McGinn. Emily fired up her vehicle without turning on her lights. Surveillance in an unfamiliar location was less than ideal, especially in a place like Berera. Even though she tagged McGinn's SUV with a tracking device, Emily couldn't count on it due to the shoddy cell coverage that powered the GPS.

She kept her distance but never lost sight of them. In a way, it was a metaphor for how she felt about Hawk ever since that day in Jordan when she was torn from him. Despite her willingness to go along with the plan, it wasn't her preference. She minced no words when she expressed to her superiors that the method seemed over the top and cruel. They ignored her suggestions, and she caved.

Hawk's cries still haunted her, even more so since he finally learned the truth about what happened that day. They could've extracted her much more quietly, though at the time she didn't realize she was being used as a pawn in a larger scheme. A simple transfer would've sufficed to get her out of Jordan. Instead, it was a big show, all designed to stir up Hawk and use him as a weapon. They just never counted on the fact that he might jilt them.

She managed to keep up yet avoid detection when McGinn's vehicle finally came to a stop outside a warehouse dock. Once she turned off the engine, Emily watched Hawk step into the street and then climb over a fence with ease. It was as if he was made for this type of work, a far cry from the compassionate American he portended to be when she first met him several years ago. As Hawk slipped into the shadows, Emily knew her mission would fail. Trying to convince a man that the pathway to his destiny should take a dramatic detour wasn't an easy sell. She knew it would be impossible.

Just getting a message to Hawk almost proved to be too much for Emily. She wanted to steal across the street and tuck a note beneath the windshield wiper. But it was too risky. She might get caught delivering the note—or he might get caught reading it. Either way, she couldn't identify any safe opportunity.

For several minutes, Emily sat in her car, paralyzed by fear. She refused to tempt fate not once but twice in delivering the message. If she were to get caught, she had no obvious allies. If McGinn caught Hawk, she was unsure of what might become of him. She bit delicately around her thumbnail, trimming it until it became smooth. After a few moments more of deliberation about what to do, she turned on her car and drove away.

Emily dialed Parker's number.

"Did you speak to him yet?" Parker asked.

"This isn't as easy as you might imagine," Emily said. "I can't just convince him to meet me for coffee and go hand him a note."

"Well, you better figure out a way fast, because he's running out of time and—"

"Come on, Parker. Can't you be more patient?"

"In this case, you're the one running out of time since you seem to be the only person around here who thinks he can be persuaded to join us. And be honest with me, do you even really think he can be convinced at this point?"

Emily sighed. "I'm hopeful."

"You've always been a terrible liar. He gets until Sunday to decide. After that, I can make him no promises regarding what will happen to him next."

"Fine. I'll figure a way."

"It's no skin off my chin, either way, though I'd prefer to have him join us than eliminate him."

"I understand."

"Good luck, Emily."

She hung up and exhaled.

Emily knew Hawk would never come around, but she at least wanted to try—and give him a heads up that someone would soon be going after him.

CHAPTER 12

ALEX WATCHED McGINN CLIMB up a chain-link fence before hoisting himself up onto the roof of a small utility shed just over the other side. Hawk insisted that she follow McGinn so she'd be able to escape with him in the event that someone stumbled upon them. She took a deep breath and followed McGinn's path to the top. Hawk joined them a few moments later, and McGinn began to share his plan.

"That warehouse is where everything is supposed to go down," McGinn said, pointing to the building adjacent to where they were standing. "Inside there are a few spots where we can create a kill box, and I think the best one is right near the exit."

"Let's see it," Hawk said.

Alex trailed behind the two men as they talked strategy for how they would cordon off the men who would deliver the chemical weapon to the boat at the docks. She watched the pale half moon on the horizon flash in and out of view due to the sporadic clouds drifting across the sky. Lights flashed and flickered on various watercraft all along the docks. Less than a mile from shore, she counted six boats returning to the harbor.

"What are you going to do about all the activity around here?" she interrupted to ask McGinn. "It's not like you'll be able to avoid detection."

"The weekends here are quiet. All the crewmen are home getting drunk and trying to pick up a woman at a bar somewhere. I could set this whole dock on fire, and nobody would notice until Monday."

"If you say so," she said.

"Don't worry. We won't need to make a lot of noise to get what we're coming here for."

"I hope you're right."

"When have I been wrong?"

Alex chuckled to herself and kept following as they crept across the rooftops until they reached the area McGinn had spoke about.

"Alex, just below us is the place where you can tap into the security feed," McGinn said. "We'll try to take care of that as soon as possible. Go check it out."

Alex wasn't sure she wanted to leave them. "I'd rather not go alone, since I'm unarmed."

McGinn yanked up his pants leg, revealing an ankle holster. He jerked the gun out and handed it to her. "Now you're armed."

Alex took the gun and tucked it into the back of her pants. She shimmied down a light pole positioned a few feet away from the edge of the roof. Once she reached the ground, she located a locked gray box that had a series of wires running all around it. She inspected the wires before she jimmied the lock open. Inside, she saw a network of video cables and other wires. McGinn knew the layout of the building well and made it clear to Alex that it was her job to make sure nobody was surprised on Saturday night when the exchange occurred.

Once Alex finished inspecting the box, she climbed back on top of the roof and rejoined Hawk and McGinn. The two men were crouched down, peering inside a skylight.

"What are we looking at?" she asked.

"This is where the exchange is going down," McGinn said. "Get a good look, because when you're staring at the closed-circuit video feeds, we need to make sure this room is monitored closely."

"Does it need to be empty?" she asked.

"No. We just need to know how many people are inside," McGinn said. "We're going to turn this room into a kill box once we identify who has the weapon."

"How exactly do you plan to get out?" Hawk asked.

McGinn pointed at the far wall. "There are

windows on both sides that are easily accessible. Do you see them?"

Hawk nodded. "They seem a bit high off the ground."

"Well, easily accessible with the aid of a table or chair."

Alex expressed her reservations. "That may not be so easy to get to if other gunmen enter the room. You'd be sitting targets then."

McGinn turned around and looked at Alex, flashing a wry grin. "That's why we're going to secure the room first. No one gets in until we get out."

"If you think this is the best plan of attack, I'm willing to go along with it," Hawk said.

"You got any better ideas?" McGinn sneered.

"This is your turf," Hawk said. "Don't take any offense. If I were running this op, I'd prefer to have a better backup plan. But I'm deferring to you here."

"Good," McGinn said. "What about you, sweetheart? You want to mount your high horse and tell me what a horrible idea this is?"

Alex shook her head. "I'll be able to handle what you've asked for. If you think you can get the job done with this plan, let's do it."

They all headed toward the alleyway where they'd parked. When McGinn was a good ten meters ahead, Alex leaned in to Hawk.

"I'm beginning to wonder if this guy has ever planned an operation in his entire life," she said. "He's overly confident for such a flimsy plan. Everything has to go just right for this to play out like he hopes."

"Just keep your head down and do your job," Hawk said. "And have an escape route in case things go sideways—because they just might. We need to set up a rendezvous point in case we get separated during the mission."

Alex nodded. "We do. We also need to talk about something else that I learned about our host."

"What is it?" he asked.

"Can't talk about it now, but we need to—and soon."

They crouched near the edge of the roof and waited for the guards to make their rounds and clear the area. Once they did, the trio climbed down and returned to their vehicle, McGinn wasted little time in firing up the engine and stomping on the gas. The tires barked as the car accelerated.

"That's not exactly the best way to avoid being seen," Hawk said.

McGinn laughed him off. "Did you see anyone there when we left?"

"No, but—"

"Exactly. These are a bunch of knuckleheads who would have a hard time tracking down anyone who attacked them in broad daylight in a confined space. Did you see how easy it was for us to get in and out of there?"

Hawk shifted in his seat as he glanced over his shoulder. "You can never be too careful."

McGinn snickered. "These guys are hacks. It took me less than a week of recon to figure out how we were going to stop this exchange from taking place."

"Why didn't you just do it yourself?" Alex snipped.

"Just because it's easy, sweetheart, doesn't mean I can do it alone."

Alex bit her tongue, seething at his blatant patronization.

"Take a right up here," Hawk said.

McGinn shot Hawk a look. "What the hell for? Gotta pick up someone?"

"I think we're being followed."

McGinn chuckled again and shook his head. "I ask for the best and brightest, and this is what I get."

"Two highly-trained and accomplished operatives? I'd say you got exactly what you asked for," Alex said.

"The jury's still out on that," McGinn said before jerking the steering wheel to the right and rounding the corner.

They raced along the surface streets for over a minute without seeing another car on the road. McGinn finally broke the awkward silence.

"You satisfied now that no one is trailing us?"

Hawk took a deep breath and glanced over his shoulder through the back window. A pair of headlights could be seen in the distance.

"That other car is still back there."

McGinn abruptly pulled the car over to the side of the road and shoved the gear into park. The car that had been behind them roared past and kept going.

"See—what did I tell you?" he said. "Nobody's tailing us, so chill out, okay?"

Alex looked through the back window and saw a pair of highlights in the distance.

McGinn looked at her through the rearview mirror. "Turnaround, toots. I just proved there's nobody back there tailing us. Now, let's stay focused on the task at hand."

CHAPTER 13

HASSAN GARAAR WOKE UP EARLY Thursday morning and began another round of quality control checks on his sarin. He donned his hazmat suit and siphoned out a small amount of the liquid onto a petri dish and slid it under the microscope. All the molecules still appeared stable. But he wasn't satisfied with a simple inspection; he required a demonstration for peace of mind.

Garaar grabbed one of the mice from the terrarium in his office, placing the feisty animal inside a sealed room where he could vaporize the gas. A couple small puffs later, Garaar peered through the window and watched the animal twitch and turn until it gasped its last breath.

Everything is working properly.

Garaar took pride in fighting for the cause he signed up to protect, but it wasn't the only reason he was excited about seeing the sarin leave his hands.

Garaar was also thrilled about what was going to be placed in his hands—money, and plenty of it.

During his time studying at Caltech, Garaar began to see how Americans could enjoy such a culture. For as long as he could remember, he heard about how morally debased the United States was. His grandfather once told him that the country was full of whores. "Men can't even walk down the street without a woman throwing herself at him," Garaar's grandfather explained. "These women are on every corner with one goal—and that is to take you down." Those words haunted Garaar, even to the point that he almost reneged at the last moment on his pledge to attend Caltech so he could help out Al-Shabaab. But his commitment to the cause ultimately triumphed.

While at Caltech, Garaar discovered that his grandfather either didn't know what he was talking about or things had dramatically changed. Garaar found it nearly impossible to get a woman to talk to him. Despite the fact that the overwhelming majority of his classmates were male, Garaar wondered why women wouldn't speak to him. He desperately wanted to fit in and wanted to make the best of the next four to five years of his life. But he seemed resigned to the fact that being *one of the guys* would have to happen without having a girlfriend.

Before he accepted that reality, Garaar questioned if anything was wrong with him. He asked his friends, classmates, roommates—anyone who would speak with him—if there was anything about him that was keeping women from talking to him. He received a wide array of advice, varying from fashion tips to ways to engage a woman in conversation. He tried it all, and none of it worked.

However, Garaar watched in amazement as Theodore Holdman seemed to need a security team to keep women away from him. Theodore, who was affectionately called Teddy Bear by those closest to him, quickly became the most desirable man on campus. But his ability to attract women extended beyond the Caltech campus boundaries and reached neighboring UCLA. At one point in the spring of Garaar's freshman year, Teddy Bear was dating a UCLA cheerleader and became a school legend.

But Garaar couldn't figure out why. Teddy Bear wasn't overweight, but he certainly wasn't a jock. He wore dark rimmed glasses and rarely combed his hair. His fashion of choice—solid color cardigans—were often accessorized with mustard and ketchup stains. For a few weeks, Teddy Bear even grew a splotchy mustache that seemed to have no effect on the women who flocked to him. Garaar watched in awe until he finally asked one of his roommates about the

Theodore Holdman phenomena.

"You think Theodore Holdman has some secret trick to getting babes?" Garaar's roommate asked as he started to chuckle. "There are two billion tricks he has, if you know what I mean."

Garaar cocked his head to one side. "Two billion tricks?"

"Tricks equal dollars, dope. Ever heard of Holdman Financial Holdings?"

Garaar shook his head.

"That's the company where the elite in this country go when they want to invest. And Theodore is set to inherit his father's business when he retires."

"But he's studying engineering here."

"Yes, computer engineering, which he's doing so he can better research the industry for his father's company. He already has a business degree that he got from USC when he was eighteen."

Garaar nodded slowly. "I see. So, it's all about the money?"

His roommate laughed. "That's an understatement. Chicks would dig you too if you had money."

It was an off-handed comment, but one that stuck with Garaar. He desperately wanted a woman—or a whole bunch of them like Holdman. It didn't matter. Garaar was convinced it'd help him fit in better.

However, it didn't seem to matter as Garaar failed time after time in his attempts to lure women to going on more than one date with him. He only got two first dates, which both ended abruptly before the evening was finished. It left Garaar more determined than ever to win over the heart of a woman—and it had to be an American woman. His family could pick a Muslim for him to marry at any point. But Garaar wanted to woo one on his own.

When Garaar entered the world of online dating, he found it easy to be someone else. The profile he created made outlandish claims. He was a business mogul from the Middle East who'd amassed a fortune in oil. He took pictures of himself next to yachts with a drink in his hand to enhance the illusion. Then he began his search. It wasn't long until he found a sucker, a woman who lapped up every outrageous story he fabricated and shared with her as if it were the truth. However, something troubling happened along the way: Garaar started to actually like the woman.

Cindy Freeman from Miami, Florida, wasn't just another American woman whose heart he wanted to conquer; Garaar wanted to share his heart with hers. He knew it sounded insane, but it was how he felt. He went from simply getting a woman to like him online to wanting her in real life—and he couldn't do it without being a fraud … unless he could find a way to become rich.

After months and months of talk, Cindy told Garaar that if he didn't come over and meet her—because if he was that rich, what could stop him, she said—she was going to move on. She expressed his desire to connect in person and see if a future was possible. Then Garaar said he'd meet her on his yacht once he was able to work out the details.

She gave him a month at the time and extended it two weeks when Garaar asked for it. When he asked again, she refused and gave him the ultimatum. Garaar wasn't sure he could pull it off, but when the opportunity to make a ton of money by selling the sarin to the Al Hasib, he began to believe it was possible. That's when he started talking up his wealth more than he should have. He swallowed hard with every new lie that he told. Instead of tamping down the lies, he ramped them up, justifying it all by convincing himself that it would all be true once he sold the Sarin.

Almost there.

Garaar smiled as he scrolled through the list of yachts for sale on a used boat website. He'd already picked out the one he wanted and contacted the owner. In a few short days, he'd be standing on the dock in the picture and waiting for Cindy to join him on board.

He logged into the dating website where he'd connected with Cindy and noticed he had a message from her.

**I'm starting to think you're making this all up.
I want to see you ASAP.**

He stared at the computer screen for a moment and took a deep breath.

Saturday can't get here soon enough. But maybe it doesn't have to.

Garaar dialed the number of Rashid Qureshi, the Al Hasib agent who was supposed to collect the Sarin.

"It's not a good idea to be calling me," Qureshi said.

"I know, but I was wondering if you wanted to accelerate our timetable by one day," Garaar said.

"Is there a problem?"

"I just thought—"

"Is there a problem?"

"No, but I just—"

"I'll see you at the time and place we originally scheduled. Do not contact me again under any circumstances. Do you understand?"

"Yes," Garaar mumbled as he hung up.

With just under sixty hours until the exchange was scheduled to go down, Garaar wondered if he could last that long. He wanted to lock himself into a room and come out when it was time to make the deal.

Garaar hoped Cindy would understand.

CHAPTER 14

HAWK HAD SLEPT IN worse conditions, but he didn't expect to be confined to such rudimentary lodging for so long. The attack on McGinn's compound forced them underground and understandably so. McGinn lost several men in the attack, while the ones who survived had mostly fled into hiding. It was anybody's guess if or when Al-Shabaab might strike again, and considering the damage their initial assault inflicted, nobody wanted to be around for a second one.

The threadbare blanket Hawk pulled tight against his body provided little protection from the constant draft in the basement. If it hadn't been against mission protocol, he would've considered inviting Alex to join him; yet with McGinn in the room, it would've made an awkward sleeping arrangement even more so. The first rays of sunlight trickled through the cracks in the wooden floor above them and signaled to Hawk that it was time to get up.

He rolled off the cot and pressed his feet firmly against the cold floor. He shivered and wrapped a blanket around his shoulders.

"Chilly in the basement, ain't it, cowboy?" McGinn said.

Hawk glanced in the direction of McGinn and nodded.

"In about an hour, you'll probably be able to fry an egg on the concrete," McGinn said. "But down here? It'll make you question that you're in one of the warmest cities in the world."

Hawk shook his head. "Is there an air conditioner that I'm not aware of?"

"You're funny. You know that? This is Somalia. As far as these people know, air conditioning hasn't even been invented yet."

Hawk sniffed the air and then zeroed in on the cup in McGinn's hand.

"Where'd you get that?" Hawk asked.

McGinn grinned. "Coffee isn't easy to come by this early in the morning, but I slipped out and got some equipment for Alex to make sure she'll have everything she needs for Saturday night. And while I did, I grabbed some coffee too. Want some?"

Hawk nodded.

"Too bad," McGinn said, laughing. "I didn't have

enough hands to carry more than one cup."

Alex sat up and pushed the hair out of her eyes. "You're an asshole, McGinn."

"And good morning to you too, buttercup," McGinn shot back. "I come bearing gifts that would make Santa Claus blush in shame, yet the first words out of your mouth are disparaging toward me. What gives?"

"I'm gonna give you a piece of my mind if you continue your pretentious act," she said. "I want my equipment and a cup of coffee."

"Will it make you behave more civilly?"

Alex glared at McGinn.

He threw his hands in the air. "Okay, okay. You win. I brought cups of coffee for both of you." He distributed a cup each to Hawk and Alex. "You could be a little nicer, you know?"

Alex glared at McGinn and took a swig of the coffee. She immediately doubled over, pretending as if she was about to vomit.

"What'd you use to filter this with? A dirty sock that had been tucked away in a locker for years?"

McGinn smiled. "Must've finally switched out that filter." He put his hand up to the side of his face as if he were about to tell a secret. "You should've had some coffee from the last batch."

"Forget it," she said. "Just give me the equipment."

"Fine," McGinn said, gesturing toward the corner of the room, where a stack of electronic gadgets sat. "Everything you need for Saturday night."

Hawk watched as Alex flung off her covers and shuffled across the room.

"What about the muscle?" Hawk asked.

"The muscle? You're it, cowboy," McGinn said.

"I'm talking about the guns. This isn't likely to be the picnic you think it's going to be. When the bad guys have guns, they shoot back."

McGinn rolled his eyes and stood up. "Look, you'll have everything you need. I promise."

"That's not a satisfactory answer. I need to see what I'm dealing with and make sure every weapon I have is going to operate the way it's supposed to if you expect me to assist you."

"I couldn't bring everything back here," McGinn said. "At least, I couldn't do it in broad daylight."

"This isn't an option for me," Hawk said. "I need to see what's at my disposal."

McGinn dug a keychain out of his pants pocket and tossed it at Hawk. "Why don't you go get it yourself?"

Hawk glared at him. "I have no idea where I'm supposed to go."

"I'll give you directions and the combination to the safe. It'll be like an early Christmas for you. I promise."

"And you'll stay here and take care of Alex?"

McGinn rolled his eyes. "Geez, man, she's a grown woman. I think she can handle pretty much anything that's thrown her way."

"I don't want her left alone. We're a team."

"Oh, God, just go, will you? I promise I won't leave. Just promise me you will."

Hawk nodded.

McGinn drew up directions for how to find the compound and where the weapons were located.

"Why can't we just use the tunnels?" Hawk finally asked.

"What if someone sees you? We're all dead then. Use the truck. It's all clear at the compound for now. Nobody is watching the place."

"Yet, we're still here, hiding out," Hawk snapped.

"Only to be cautious. Trust me, nobody is there now."

Hawk sighed and shook his head. "I hope you're right. I'd hate to leave more carnage at your compound."

"Do what you must."

Hawk walked upstairs, intruding upon the startled old woman's morning routine. Her eyes widened as she looked at Hawk.

"It's okay," Hawk said. "I'm a guest of Mr. McGinn."

She forced a smile and nodded.

Hawk figured the mention of McGinn's name put her at ease, though he was far from it. Once he stepped into the warm Berera air, he started to wonder if McGinn was the worst operative the CIA had ever commissioned into the field.

The drive back to the compound took no more than five minutes. When Hawk arrived at the gate, he stepped out of the truck and looked around. It was just as McGinn had promised. Stillness in the morning. Nobody was walking along the walls of the compound. There wasn't a soul left to guard anything inside. The only thing between a weapons cache and the outside world were a pair of doors that were tenuously held together by a security system. Hawk had the keys to unlock the gate, but he imagined that anyone determined enough could break inside. And it was only a matter of time before someone actually did that.

Hawk typed in a code on the keypad, and the gate swung open. Returning to his vehicle, he slid into the driver's side and eased onto the gas. Once inside, the doors shut behind him.

Jamming the car into park, Hawk drove toward the area McGinn had marked on his map. All the weapons they'd ever need were allegedly inside a hidden room at the end of the barracks. Hawk didn't want to waste any time getting a peek inside them either.

Hawk parked and sprinted toward the door to the barracks. He entered another code that McGinn had given and wasted no time finding the door to the room he had mentioned. Inside, it was a literal treasure trove of weapons. Plenty of bullets that matched the types of guns harbored inside. Handguns and sniper rifles and everything else in between.

I need you and you and you and ...

Hawk smiled as he snatched everything he could hold in his hands before shoveling the weapons and ammo into the back of McGinn's SUV. He scanned the area, which was devoid of any activity, and got inside the truck.

After some time to reflect on McGinn's plan, Hawk concluded it was solid, but not perfect. If it were up to him, he would have a better escape route. No matter how committed he was to the mission, staying alive was always the component he considered first if the threat to thousands of lives was imminent. And danger was lurking at some point in the near future. He preferred to live to die another day, as cliché as that approach was to his work. But having enough weapons to fend off a small army for several hours eased Hawk's concerns. He knew he could fight his way out of any situation if properly supplied. He glanced at the weapons in the back and smiled as he nodded.

That's enough to get me and Alex out alive if McGinn's plan falls apart.

When Hawk whipped his head back around, he almost didn't see the vehicle stopped in front of him. Hawk stomped on the brakes as the SUV slid to a stop. As he started to pull around the car, a woman got out and gestured for him to halt.

What the hell?

It was Emily.

Hawk looked in the back and flung a blanket over the guns and munitions before getting out.

"What are you doing here?" Hawk asked as he approached his former girlfriend.

"I would ask you the same thing, but I already know."

"Just get in the car with me. We need to talk."

Hawk pulled his vehicle over to the side of the road and locked it.

"This better not take long," he said. "I need to get back or some people might come looking for you."

"That idiot you're working with couldn't find his head if it wasn't attached to his neck."

Hawk got into the car with Emily. "What's so important that you had to follow me halfway across the world?"

"I had to ask you one more time to come work for Searchlight and—"

"Come on, Emily. You know that's not gonna happen."

"Well, that was only half the reason I came to ask you in person."

"You couldn't just give me a call?"

"No, because they're always listening."

"Who? Searchlight?"

She nodded and put the car in drive before easing onto the gas and moving forward.

"That's comforting," Hawk said.

"If you don't acquiesce to their demands, Hawk, they're going to come after you."

Hawk eyed her closely. "Come after me? What do you mean?"

"I mean, they're going to kill you. They see you as a threat. And that's what they do to the enemies. If you don't join them, they will take you out."

"Good," Hawk said as a wry grin spread across his face. "I'd much rather know where someone stands than have them pussyfooting around the truth."

"You don't understand. They're not going to stop until you're dead."

"Then they're gravely underestimating what I can do."

"Listen, Hawk, there's more to it than this.

There's—"

Instead of another word, all Hawk heard was the crunching of metal as his head snapped forward and then back against the passenger side window.

That was the last thing he remembered before everything went dark.

CHAPTER 15

J.D. BLUNT DONNED his best disguise—a fedora and oversized glasses—and ventured into the market in Tangier. He hated the crowds crammed into tight spaces. It was a street thief's dream. Blunt always kept at least one hand in his pocket, clutching his wallet. He only made the mistake once as a couple of savvy kids ran a distract-and-snatch scheme that began a two-day descent into bureaucracy hell trying to get a new ID and credit cards. He vowed it would never happen again.

While Blunt loathed the market environment, he enjoyed the unbridled nature of people selling their wares of all shapes and sizes out in the open. Blunt chewed on his cigar as he stopped and looked at the woman displaying handmade necklaces and bracelets along with fresh eggs. The man next to her was selling pirated DVD copies of blockbuster movies along with kitchen utensils. It was as if a bomb exploded in

Wal-Mart and nobody bothered to reorganize the store.

He shuffled through the crowd, his left hand firmly grasping his wallet, while his right clutched a cane. While he didn't need it to walk, Blunt used the cane as much to engender sympathy and elderly respect as he did to create breathing room amid the masses. Tapping his cane on the cobblestone street as he drifted past one desperate salesperson to the next, Blunt finally found his store run by his man, Amir.

"What brings my favorite customer back here on this fine day?" Amir asked.

"Amir, I'm only your favorite because I'm the only one who has any money."

Amir laughed and ripped off a few crumbs of bread for his pet monkey, Aman. "You know me too well, Mr. Texas Man. You know me too well."

Blunt was certain that Amir's name was something else; it's why Blunt never used his real name in dealing with the street vendor.

"So, what can I do for you, Mr. Texas Man?"

"I need a camera."

"Like this?" Amir said as he stooped down and picked up a point-and-shoot digital camera.

Blunt shook his head. "I'm thinking more along the lines of a small web camera, the kind I can install and view from my phone?"

A smile broke across Amir's face as he shook his finger at Blunt. "I never suspected you to be that kind of guy, Mr. Texas Man."

Blunt bit hard on his cigar, grinding it between his teeth. "I'm not a pervert, Amir, if that's what you're implying."

Amir disappeared for a moment behind a curtain at the back of his booth. He emerged carrying a small box.

"I am not here to judge, only to serve the needs of my customers," Amir said as he handed the box to Blunt.

Blunt took it. "What do I owe you?"

"Five hundred U.S. dollars."

"Five hundred? Are you out of your mind?"

Amir shrugged. "That is my price. If you know of another store where you can purchase such an item, I suggest you go there instead."

"Three hundred fifty and not a penny more," Blunt said.

"Four hundred and it's yours," Amir countered.

Blunt grunted and fished out the money from his wallet. He handed it to Amir, who smiled big as he took it.

"You are an extortionist," Blunt said.

"I have mouths to feed, children to clothe, a wife to make happy."

Blunt turned and walked away, hoisting his cane in the air, the box tucked snug up against his body with his left arm.

"See you soon, Amir."

Blunt stepped back into the current of the crowd drifting along the main thoroughfare. A couple boys bumped into him as they ran by, knocking Blunt off balance. As he started to tumble, one of the boys snatched the box and started to run. Blunt, however, regained his balance and use the crook of his cane to hook the boy's right ankle and send him sprawling to the ground. Blunt knelt down and picked up his box. He looked into the boy's eyes, which appeared to tremble.

"Pick on someone your own age," Blunt said before he stepped over the boy and continued along.

Blunt was ready to get back to his room and relax, but not until he installed the camera. He couldn't truly relax until he finished, and even then, could he actually relax? He doubted it, but it was worth a try.

Blunt's phone buzzed, interrupting his train of thought about how he was going to install the camera. He would've ignored it altogether if it hadn't been for the caller's name pasted across the front of his screen. It was someone he hadn't talked to in a while but needed to for the sake of his own security as well as his operatives'.

It was General Johnson.

CHAPTER 16

ALEX WATCHED THE DAYLIGHT spilling through the cracks in the floor turn faint as the hours ticked past. She supposed Hawk shouldn't have been gone more than half an hour, yet darkness was about to set in and still no word from him. She grew annoyed at McGinn's apathetic response to Hawk's absence.

"Aren't you going to do something?" she asked, huffing after she did.

"Do what? I've already told you the first twenty times you asked that question that I can't really do anything without jeopardizing this mission."

"Don't you get it?" Alex said. "There isn't going to be a mission without Hawk. You can't stay here forever. You've got no idea what's going on in the real world up there right now. We're just two caged little animals, though I'm clearly more upset with this arrangement than you are."

"Simmer down, princess. I'm sure your cowboy

hero will return any moment now."

"You've been saying that several hours now, and it hasn't happened yet."

McGinn growled. "Fine. I'll go check on him. But you stay here and keep your prying little eyes to yourself. I'll know if you looked at something."

He glanced up at the lights. She hadn't even considered that McGinn had surveillance in the room.

McGinn put on his cap and opened the door to the tunnels. He had almost exited the room entirely before he turned around and poked his head back inside.

"Don't worry. I'll be back soon," he said.

"I'll be waiting for you, *dear*," Alex said with an exaggerated eye roll.

Alex listened until his footsteps faded down the tunnel just outside the door. She wanted to punch herself in the face for being so careless. As careful as she was, she never considered McGinn would have placed surveillance in what amounted to a panic room in a basement. She had no one else to blame but herself.

Maybe he's not such an amateur after all.

Whether he was a professional or amateur, she didn't care; she simply needed to doctor the footage in the event that McGinn happened to review it. Or maybe someone else was watching.

Whatever the case, she needed the video gone twenty minutes ago.

CHAPTER 17

HIS EYES SLOWLY as he regained consciousness. His side ached from what he assumed was the impact of the vehicle that hit him and Emily. That was the last thing he remembered. He tried to move, but the ropes tethering him to the wooden chair prevented any serious mobility. The piece of cloth tied snug around his face tasted like a cocktail of dirt and sweat and wreaked of mold.

Due to the lack of bright light, Hawk couldn't tell how big the room was. A lone bulb dangled from the ceiling, casting an ominous shadow on him. The light's reach wasn't more than ten square feet, which left Hawk to wonder what lurked in the darkness.

"Emmm-ahhhhh-leeeeee," he tried to shout through the gag. He tried twice more with his muffled voice but to no avail. Equally concerning as her absence was the fact that his cries for her didn't seem to attract the attention of anyone. He sat in the room alone for another fifteen minutes before he heard a door swing open.

Hawk whipped his head in the direction of the sound as light from the outside flooded into the room. It was enough to give Hawk a glimpse of what kind of environment he was truly in—a stark one. No other doors nor any other exit points, with the exception of a window in the corner.

Good to know.

A medium-built man strode across the room, his hands clasped behind his back. He stopped a few feet short of Hawk and looked him up and down.

"So, this is the great Brady Hawk," the man said before breaking into laughter. "You don't look so great right now."

The man, who sported the nametag of General attached to the left side of his jacket, removed Hawk's gag.

"What's the meaning of this?" Hawk asked. "Who are you?"

The General clucked his tongue and wagged his index finger at Hawk. "I ask all the questions around here. Is that clear?"

"What was that?" Hawk said, feigning as he couldn't hear.

The General put his hands on his knees and leaned forward, stopping just inches from Hawk's face.

"I asked *is that clear?*" the man said.

Sensing an opportunity, Hawk lunged toward the General and clamped down hard on his ear. Hawk bit harder as the man squirmed in an effort to escape. As the General thrashed about, he gave Hawk all the leverage he needed to get off the ground and turn the tables on his captor. Hawk tried to maintain his balance long enough until he got into a position to let the General break a hard fall. Hawk came crashing down on the man as the chair splintered. Immediately, Hawk found himself free and grabbed the rope, but not before he snatched the General.

Hawk worked furiously to tie his new prisoner up.

"You yell for your guards and I'll break your neck right here without another thought," Hawk said. "Do *you* understand *me*?"

The man nodded.

"So, tell me General, where is she?"

"Who?"

"Don't play games with me. I know you took her—and for all I know, she was the original target."

The General chuckled and shook his head. "Oh, no. It was you all along. You were the primary target."

"Where is she then? And you better not say dead or else I'm going to rip you apart right now."

"I'll tell you," the man said. "Come closer."

Hawk edged closer but wasn't about to get as close as the man had been when Hawk summoned him.

Instead of saying something, the man spit into Hawk's eyes.

"I'll never tell you anything," the General said.

Undeterred, Hawk knelt down next to the man. "So, tell me, General, how good are you at arithmetic?"

The General seemed shocked by the question, taken aback by the oddity if not absurdity of it. "Do you mean math?"

"Yes, math. How good are you at it?"

The General smiled and shrugged. "Good enough to know your odds of making it out alive are decreasing with every second you keep me tied up here."

"Oh, I doubt that," Hawk said as he began to pace around the General. "Let's start first with some basic questions, like how many fingers do you have?"

The General started laughing and ignored the question.

"I'm serious, General," Hawk said. "How many digits do you have on your hands."

"Ten," the man finally said.

"Now, we're going to play a little game," Hawk said. "I ask a question, you tell me the answer. If you don't tell me the answer, we do a little subtraction problem."

"What's one idiot minus a brain equal?" the man said. "Give up? A dead idiot."

Hawk glared at him before picking up the man's gun off the floor that he'd lost during their initial struggle.

"I'll never tell you anything," the man said.

"I can be persuasive when I want to be," Hawk said, tapping the barrel of the gun against the palm of his hand. "So, let me ask this one more time—where is my friend?"

The man spit in Hawk's face again.

Hawk shook his head. "Subtraction it is then."

He knelt down behind the man's chair and grabbed his pinky finger. "Ten fingers minus one finger equals ..."

The man's shoulders slumped as he said nothing.

"Nine fingers," Hawk said as he ripped into the man's hand, slicing off his right pinky. "Or seven if we're being technical and classify thumbs as different appendages."

The man let out a guttural scream.

"Now where is she?" Hawk asked again. "I can do this all day long if necessary."

The General sucked in a breath through his teeth and exhaled, his face grimacing. "Okay, okay, I'll talk. She's in the building next to this one."

"I swear if you hurt her, I'll come back and kill you."

"She wasn't the target. You were."

"Me?"

"I don't even know who she is."

Hawk grabbed the man's hand again. "Who sent you?"

"I don't even know the guy's name."

Hawk narrowed his eyes. "Is that so?"

"Okay, okay. I'll tell you."

There was pounding on the door.

"Sir, are you okay?" a man shouted through the door.

"Don't say a word," Hawk said, training his gun on the man.

"I'll tell you what you want to know, but I've got say something or my guards will come crashing through the door, and you won't have a chance."

Hawk sighed. "Fine."

The man took a deep breath and shouted. "This maniac has me. Help!"

"Wrong answer," Hawk said before shooting the man in the head.

A pounding began against the door. Hawk scanned the room for the lone remaining exit—the window.

Two more thumps against the door. Hawk hustled up to the window and pushed up. It refused to budge.

He then backed up halfway across the room.

Another loud thump at the door.

Here it goes.

Hawk broke into a dead sprint for the window. He hadn't taken more than ten steps before the lock gave way and the door flung open. Despite the commotion, Hawk didn't look back, instead leaping and diving head first through the window.

As he hit the ground outside, shattered glass rained down all around him. Blood trickled down his face while the sounds of gunfire echoed from the room above. He scrambled to his feet and tried to get his bearings.

Looking around the compound, his concern for Emily grew.

There was no other building.

CHAPTER 18

THE BIGGEST CHALLENGE facing Alex was finding the location of the storage device. She inspected the camera lodged in the light fixture and determined it was wireless, leading her to believe it was likely still in the room. She checked the room's lone closet to find nothing but clothes strewn about, most drooping halfway off hangers. She paced around the room, looking for a spot in the floor where McGinn could hide the device. But there wasn't anything readily apparent.

Alex then resorted to tapping the wall in search of a hollow area. When that yielded no results, she removed the two pictures from the wall.

There you are.

Alex smiled and found a black metal box with blinking lights that was plugged into a special electrical outlet built into the hidden area. She carefully rotated the box toward her and found a small screen on the back. After a few seconds of fiddling with the controls, she managed to turn on the screen. A navigational bar appeared at the top, allowing her to scroll through previous day's recordings. The fact that the device was motion activated made it easy for her to eliminate the images of her without drawing too much suspicion.

Alex deleted all the images up until the day she first walked into the room. In a perfect scenario, she would've deleted more so that it didn't seem so coincidental that the camera stopped recording the day she arrived there. However, she knew that if she deleted a few weeks prior to when she and Hawk came to Berera and McGinn had checked the footage during that time, she would've been busted for sure. At least the current situation gave her the chance to talk her way out of a situation.

She was about to put the box back in place but decided to snoop around on it for a few more minutes. Refusing her curiosity was next to impossible, no matter how dangerous the situation, which was why she was hacking into the security feed in the first place. She smiled and shrugged before continuing to poke through the device. It wasn't long before she discovered a large archive with little of interest. Then she pushed another button that opened another archive—at least that's what she thought it was at first.

Alex quickly realized it actually wasn't another archive; it was a live feed, and she could see McGinn.

"What are you up to, you little weasel?" she asked aloud.

She pushed another button, revealing a different camera angle. Another button and then another camera.

Alex leaned close to the screen and squinted. The image in the background looked like the weapon they were supposed to be retrieving. She scrolled through the images again, confirming her suspicions.

He's at the warehouse where we're making the exchange. What does he need me for? He's already tapped into the feed.

She swallowed hard as another thought percolated.

Or maybe something else is going on here.

If he had wanted to kill Hawk and Alex, McGinn could've done it a long time ago. But she'd never felt easy around McGinn from the moment she met him. She needed to talk to Hawk about this, not to mention the other documents she'd found, and time was running out. An opportunity to confide in Hawk about these revelations had yet to present itself. And for the moment, she didn't even know where Hawk was.

CHAPTER 19

EMILY REFUSED TO ACCEPT her fate as four guards surrounded her. Handcuffed to a pipe running over her head, Emily's body was stretched far beyond comfort. Her feet were planted firmly on the ground, but her arms extended upward as the blood drained down, causing a tingling sensation in her hands and fingers. The skin around her wrists had been rubbed raw as she struggled to find a moment to relax.

"Allah has been good to us," one of the men said.

"No," another man said with a grin spreading wide across his face. "The General has been good to us, allowing us to indulge in some of the spoils of battle."

"I'm not a spoil, you asshole," Emily said. "I'm a woman."

The guard shrugged. "Woman … spoil of war … person to pleasure me … all the same in my book."

Emily tried to restrain her tongue, but she

couldn't. Not that it would matter. She knew where this was headed, and she figured she might as well make it as unpleasant as possible for the guards.

"You have a book? You know how to read?" she said, sneering at the man.

"You think your insults are going to bother me?" the guard asked. "I like my women feisty, especially American women."

Emily snickered. "I bet the only type of woman you've ever had are the kind you had to—"

Whack!

The guard backhanded Emily in the face. "I suggest you keep quiet."

"I thought you just said you liked your women feisty."

Holding up his index finger, the guard wagged it at Emily. "I said feisty, not dead."

"Oh, I'm very much alive. And I'm going to kill you in a few minutes."

All four of the guards broke into laughter.

"I wasn't joking," she said.

One of the other guards, who'd been looking Emily up and down while licking his lips, spoke up. "I'd like to go first—break her in."

"Trust me," she said. "You don't want to do that. It simply means you'll be the first to die."

The guard walked up to her and threw his head

back, breaking into a guffaw. He then ripped her blouse open.

"Touch me again, and it'll be the last thing you ever do."

The guard smiled. "I love it when you talk dirty to me."

Emily yanked down hard, freeing her wrists from the cuffs. Pulling up on the bar over her head, she brought her knees up even with the guard's head and wrapped her legs around him. The other guards started pointing and laughing. Based on their reactions, Emily was quite certain that not a single guard in the room had any idea they were all about to die.

After a quick twist of her legs, she heard the guard's neck crack. He crumpled to the floor in a heap.

"Who's next?" she asked as she approached the guard who'd been in charge for most of her detention.

The guard whipped his gun out and pressed the barrel of it into Emily's chest. "I think you are."

In one swift move, Emily pushed the man's hands aside, forcing him to point directly at one of the other guards. Emily eased her finger onto the man's trigger finger.

"On the count of three," she said. "One . . . "

The gun ignited as she helped the guard pull the trigger, sending a bullet into the chest of one of the other guards. The guard who'd been holding the gun scrambled away from Emily.

"Don't think I'm finished with you yet," Emily said.

She proceeded to kick him in the head, knocking him out cold. In all the commotion, she'd lost sight of the fourth guard. Scanning the room to find him, she didn't see him.

"I hate playing games," she said.

"So do I," he said from behind her.

The guard shoved a gun into her back with one hand and wrapped his arm around her neck.

"We can make this be quick and painless or slow and agonizing," he said. "It's up to you. But before any of this goes down, you're going to give me what I want."

"Really, it's up to you," Emily said. "Just depends on how you want to die."

"Hey, lady, maybe you've forgotten who's holding you down and jamming a gun into your back."

"I'm more concerned with where the bullets are going to go—and every last one of them is headed for your body."

The man started to laugh, though he tightened his grip and whispered in her ear. "Is it difficult to get through life as a stupid as you are?"

The crack of a gunshot echoed through room as

the guard collapsed to the floor. He quivered for a moment and attempted to say something unintelligible. She stepped on his arm and stooped down to pry the gun out of his hand.

"From the looks of things, you didn't really need my help," Hawk said.

Emily stood back up and glanced at him before looking back down at the dead guard.

"Nice shot, but I could've handled him. So, how do we get out of this place?"

"Aren't you the least bit curious as to why these people targeted us?"

She walked toward him. "Quite frankly, we don't have that much time right now, but I happen to already know why."

"Please enlighten me," Hawk said as he crossed his arms.

"They were after you."

"So I was told. It seems like the whole world is after me these days."

She nodded. "It seems that way because that's reality. Everyone is after you. Now, are we getting out of here or just standing around talking all day?"

"This ought to be fun. I had to fight my way out and in to this building earlier. The General told me that you were in another building when in fact you were down the hall."

"Never believe a man who wears a generic nametag with the word *General* on it."

"Lesson learned. Now, follow me. We're not out of danger yet."

She followed Hawk out of the room and hadn't hustled more than ten meters down the hall before they heard a clatter of footsteps behind them.

CHAPTER 20

GARAAR LOCKED THE DOOR as his visitor left. He walked over to his desk and scrolled through all the exterior security cameras. Other than his guest walking to his car and driving away, there was nothing to see. It was quiet and calm as late afternoon sun began to sink on the horizon.

If only things stay this way between now and Saturday night.

Garaar opened his email and responded to Cindy's note.

Will Monday be soon enough? I have to complete a multi-million dollar acquisition in Africa on Saturday.

Garaar had learned plenty at Caltech, far more than how to make Sarin. He'd learned how to craft statements sure to garner the awe and adoration of those who he sought to impress, particularly over social media or email. For a moment, he stared at the screen, admiring his work. He didn't anticipate such a quick response from Cindy. It wasn't even 9:00 a.m. in Miami where the self-proclaimed party girl lived. Perhaps she was lying about where she lived or her party lifestyle—or both.

Can't wait. Will I get to take a ride on your yacht?

Garaar glanced over at the room where the Sarin was locked away. He smiled and nodded while he typed.

Absolutely!

While Garaar was convinced Cindy was the hottest woman he'd ever had a chance of being with, he wasn't too concerned about the optimistic comments he was making, which could turn from tenuous to outright lies. If anything went wrong, Garaar would be punished severely for it at the hands of Cindy, who he assumed wouldn't be forgiving. Garaar chuckled at the thought of telling her the truth: Sorry, Cindy, I don't have a yacht. I was going to purchase one before my pending sale of chemical weapons soured. Sorry.

It wasn't an explanation women likely heard every day, but at least it was the truth. Yet, he was convinced that wasn't going to be the case. When Garaar closed his eyes, he saw himself on the deck of his new yacht, his arm around Cindy, the gentle

Atlantic waves lapping at the hull, and twinkling stars dancing above the South Florida skies. It was going to be perfect.

His phone ringing snapped him out of his fantasy.

"Is everything on track for the exchange on Saturday?" a man asked. It was Karif Fazil.

"Yes, it's just as you requested."

"Good. I hate surprises, unless I'm the one doing the surprising."

Garaar uncorked a bottle of Scotch and poured a drink. "You'll be happy to know that I spoke with the American. They won't be posing any problems."

"They? I thought there was only one CIA operative in Berbera."

"Usually, that's the case. However, there are two more agents supposed to assist him on this one."

"Is one of them named Hawk?"

"How did you—?"

"Never mind that. Just make sure you capture him. If you deliver him to me alive, I will increase your take home pay by twenty-five percent."

Garaar remained in stunned silence for a few seconds.

"Garaar? Are you there?"

He nodded vigorously, almost forgetting that he was on the phone.

128 | R.J. PATTERSON

"Garaar?" Fazil asked again.

"Oh, yes, sir. I'm still here. That's a very generous offer. I will do what I can to make sure that happens."

Garaar hung up and clicked on a Pharrell Williams album from his desktop computer. Despite an unbridled love for American music, Garaar had to be careful since returning to Africa. Not all of his friends were as open minded about certain elements of Western culture. However, Williams was one of the world's more popular artists abroad, which somehow made him more acceptable, even among the jihadists. Less than two weeks before he agreed to take the lead on making Sarin for Al-Shabaab, Garaar watched one of the executioners behead a man and then play Williams' iconic *Happy* on his phone while dancing around the camp.

Garaar stood up and paced around the room. Uncontrollable giddiness overtook him, suppressing the angst he'd felt earlier. Maybe it was the song, or the alcohol, or the anticipation of seeing Cindy. Whatever the reason, he decided not to analyze it and enjoy the moment.

If there was one thing he knew for sure, it was that when he woke up Tuesday morning, his life was going to be drastically different.

CHAPTER 21

HAWK RACED DOWN THE HALL with Emily following right behind. A quick glance over his shoulder revealed that despite the thunder of footfalls, the guards in pursuit had yet to put eyes on them. He figured the moment they did, a hail of gunfire would serve as a signal.

"In there," Hawk said, pointing to a door off to the left.

Hawk and Emily ducked inside. It was a small windowless room, no bigger than three meters square. It was dark but lit just enough to see each other's faces thanks to the light beaming into the room through the crack beneath the door.

The footsteps stopped for a moment.

"I don't think I can do what you've asked me to do," Hawk said.

"Are you sure? I think you should sleep on it some more, especially in light of what's going on right now."

"No, I'll fend for myself."

A few more seconds of silence passed with still no audible activity from the outside.

"What is this place?" Emily asked.

"It used to be a school."

"How do you know this?"

"Intel reports," he said. "I studied the area extensively. When I managed to get outside, I looked around for some landmarks and figured out where I was."

"How'd you find me?" she whispered.

Hawk put his index finger to his lips.

Footsteps roared past and continued down the hall. Hawk put his face flush with the floor to try to see if it was safe to return to exit.

"Clear?" Emily asked.

Hawk looked up and shook his head. He placed his head back down and watched the slow, methodical march of a trailing soldier. Or perhaps it was the new leader who'd taken General's place. The man moved down the hallway, checking each room by opening the doors, turning on the lights, and peeking inside.

"He's coming this way," Hawk whispered. "We're going to have to ambush him. I'll sit here in the middle of the floor. You hide behind the door. Break his arm before he shoots me."

"With pleasure," Emily said.

The guard proceeded to stop in front of their door as Hawk predicted. Hawk watched as the doorknob turned slowly. As light flooded the room from the outside, the man flipped the switch, revealing Hawk, who was sitting in a fetal position. The man smiled.

Emily shoved the door hard against the man, but it didn't throw him off balance as Hawk assumed. The guard fired one shot before Emily knocked the gun out of his hand. Hawk scrambled for it across the floor, but the man kicked it away.

Meanwhile, Emily tried to restrain the guard in order to give Hawk enough time to retrieve the gun. But the man was too strong and flung her to the ground. She landed on her back with a thud.

The guard then dove for the gun just as Hawk was about to put his hands on it. He landed on top of Hawk, pinning him to the ground, and snatched the gun.

Standing up, the man used his gun to direct Hawk to sit in the corner. Hawk followed suit and looked at Emily, who was lying prone with her head facing Hawk and turned away from the guard. She looked at Hawk and gave him a wink.

With his gun trained on Hawk, the guard yelled down the hallway in Arabic for his colleagues to join him. Hawk used the opportunity to glance around the room for something to help him knock the gun away from the man, but there wasn't anything to use.

The guard turned his full attention back on Hawk and smiled.

"We were all warned about the great Brady Hawk," the guard said. "Looks like he wasn't so great after all."

"Am I really that famous?" Hawk deadpanned.

The guard just smiled and glanced anxiously back down the hall for the men. Their footsteps were still faint but growing louder by the second.

Emily cut her eyes up at Hawk again. He gave a nod that was barely perceptible, and she swung into action.

With one explosive kick, Emily kicked the guard in his balls. As he doubled over, Hawk unleashed a vicious roundhouse kick from, rendering the man unconscious. Hawk grabbed the gun and scrambled to his feet. Emily stood up as well.

"Where to now?" she asked.

"Let's head to the room next door. We can get out through the window."

They dashed down the hall in the opposite direction of the approaching soldiers and rushed into the next room. Hawk ran over to the window and looked down.

"It's not that far of a jump," he said. "Ladies first."

Emily joined him at the window and glanced out. Without hesitating, she leapt from the second-story and rolled once she hit the ground. Gunfire echoed down the hall. Hawk glanced over his shoulder before he followed Emily.

Once he landed, they hustled across the area and hid behind the back of a car. Hawk peeked around the end to see if anyone was watching. Several men poked their heads out of the window from which Hawk and Emily had just jumped. After a few seconds, they disappeared back into the building.

"It's almost dark now, and I can't have all those weapons sitting in the car like that, if they're even still there," Hawk said.

"Are you sure you won't reconsider?" she asked.

"Searchlight is on their own as far as I'm concerned."

"They're not fooling around when they say they're going to send an assassin after you."

"And I'm not fooling around when I say that I can fend for myself. Got it?"

She nodded.

"Now, please let me get on with what I was sent here to do, and don't contact me again here."

"You're making a mistake, Hawk."

"I've made plenty of mistakes in life, and the one I've made over and over again is trusting someone else. I won't do that again."

Hawk scanned the area again before heading down the street. Based on where he was in relation to the compound, Hawk estimated he was about a ten-minute walk. He wondered if he'd ever see Emily again—or if she might be on the other side of a gun barrel if he did.

CHAPTER 22

ALEX'S EYES BULGED as Hawk descended the basement stairs carrying a large cache of weapons and munitions. After getting over her initial shock, she rushed up to him, her mouth agape.

"Where have you been?" she asked. "I was worried sick."

"I ran into some problems while I was out," he said as he dumped his load of guns onto the table.

"Someone could've seen you come in here. Are you out of your mind?"

"I doubt it. It's dark out, and the old woman who lives here didn't even notice me."

"What'd you do with McGinn's truck?"

"I parked it a block away and snuck around to the back of the house. Nobody saw me, trust me."

"My trust level is running low at the moment, so pardon me if I have just a little bit of angst about what you just did and where you were."

"Look, I really don't want to talk about it right now, but I'm fine."

Alex squinted as she studied the bruise over his right eye. She reached up to touch it, but Hawk withdrew.

"What happened there?" she asked.

"Ran into some trouble, but don't worry. I took care of it."

"Okay, I see. Going for the honest and transparent approach now, aren't we?"

Hawk ignored her jab. "Where's McGinn?"

"I sent him to look for you, so I'm assuming based on your question that you didn't run into him while he was talking to the guy who's supposedly selling the weapon to Al Hasib."

"What are you talking about?"

She open up her laptop on the table and spun the screen toward him. "I'm talking about this."

"What is this?"

"That's McGinn talking to Garaar a few hours ago at the place we're supposed to infiltrate on Saturday night. But that's not all."

Hawk's eyes widened. "Think we're being played?"

"You tell me after you have a look at these documents I found here," she said as she handed him her phone. "I took pictures of them when they were out the first time I got here. I looked for them again, but he removed them from the safe house as far as I can tell."

Hawk looked at her phone and perused the documents. "These are procedural papers for a hit, aren't they?"

"Sure looks like it to me. Look at the date."

"That's this Saturday."

Alex nodded. "Exactly. I'm not so sure about this job now. And if you want to get the hell out of here right now, I'm with you."

"Let's give him a chance to explain."

Alex stared at him slack jawed for a moment. "Are you serious? If you start putting all of this together, I'm thinking I don't want to give him any opportunity to snow us with some lie."

"So, we just let the weapon fall into Al Hasib's hands? I don't think so."

"What else do you suggest? We can't just go through with this mission like everything's fine because it isn't."

"No, but we play it cool. Maybe I'll ask him some questions, see if he comes clean. If he doesn't suspect we're on to him, McGinn's answers will be direct."

She exhaled as she shook her head. "I don't like it, but I'll go along with you on this."

"We can't abandon this mission. It's too important."

"Well, we could always steal the weapon now."

Hawk stretched his arms and walked around the room for a moment, apparently pondering Alex's idea.

"It's not a bad backup plan, but we don't need to be burning any bridges with the CIA if this is legit."

"I'm not sure it's going to matter once we leave here, Hawk. For all we know, you might already be on the CIA's hit list."

"You're probably right, but let's see how this thing plays out first."

CHAPTER 23

McGINN TOOK A DEEP BREATH, inhaling the rich aroma of Kenyan coffee brewing in a pot on the counter. He'd already drank a cup and wondered if there'd be enough for the two guests sleeping in the safe house. He called Alex just before midnight to see if Hawk had come back, explaining that he'd run into someone and had some business he needed to attend to. With Hawk back safe, she told McGinn not to worry about it and they'd talk in the morning about what happened.

McGinn arrived at the safe house at 7:00 a.m. on Friday and hoped to rouse Alex and Hawk with the smell of a hearty breakfast. Sausage, eggs, and potatoes were all sizzling in pans on the stove.

Hawk stumbled toward him, one eye open, the other still held tightly shut. "Breakfast in the morning? But you didn't even spend the night," Hawk said.

"That's how amazing I am," McGinn said with a wry grin.

Hawk sat down on a chair at the kitchen table.

McGinn placed a coffee mug in front of Hawk along with cream and sugar.

Hawk waved him off. "Real men drink coffee black."

"My grandfather said drinking it black would put hair on your chest."

Hawk studied McGinn for a few seconds. "From the looks of it, you like yours with cream and sugar."

"Be careful, Hawk. I could still spit in your eggs if you're not nice."

Hawk chuckled and took a long sip of his coffee.

"Where'd you go last night?" Hawk asked.

"I wanted to ask you the same thing," McGinn said. "I went looking for you."

Hawk smiled. "And apparently, you didn't do a very good job."

McGinn laughed and waved his spatula at Hawk. "I'm warning you. You're walking on thin ice with me." He looked in the direction of Alex, who had yet to stir. "Alex, do you want something hot to eat?"

She moaned and waved dismissively in McGinn's direction.

Hawk's smiled vanished as he turned his full attention to McGinn. "All joking aside, what happened?"

"You first," McGinn said in a more serious tone.

"I was busy with my own problems. I ran into some Al-Shabaab thugs, but I fought my way out of it."

McGinn's eyebrows shot up. "And they didn't take your weapons?"

"This isn't my first rodeo. I know how to hide my stuff from prying eyes."

"If you say so."

"I do. Now, it's your turn."

McGinn pushed the eggs around before placing the spatula down. He leaned back against the counter and crossed his arms, taking a deep breath and exhaling before he spoke.

"Like you, I was busy with my own problems."

"It had nothing to do with our heist, did it?"

McGinn shook his head. "Oh, no. Nothing like that." He paused. "I mean, nothing that's going to endanger our mission on Saturday."

"Why don't you say what you mean instead of beating around the bush with it? Did you meet with the weapons maker yesterday?"

McGinn eyed Hawk closely. "Were you following me? Is that where you were?"

Hawk laughed. "Trust me when I say this, but I would've loved to have been following you yesterday when your truck was surrounded by some of Al-Shabaab's finest who stuck their guns in my face. Yet I somehow distinctly remember *not* following you."

McGinn turned around to look at the eggs. He peeked at them, checking to see if they were ready.

"A member of the nanny state follows me here," he said as shook his head. "Just great."

"I only asked you a question. A simple yes or no would suffice."

"Okay, then. The answer is yes. Yesterday, I saw Hassan Garaar, the chemist who works for Al-Shabaab."

"Is he a close personal friend of yours?"

Turning back around, McGinn furrowed his brow and stared at Hawk. "I'm beginning to wonder if this whole mission isn't some type of a set up to bring me down."

"I can assure you that it's no such thing," Hawk countered. "I'm here to assist you; nothing more, nothing less."

"Right now, you sound quite accusatory."

"Pardon my tone, but I was simply asking you a question. There needs to be a level of trust among us if Alex and I are going to help make this mission a successful one."

"Fine. I'll lay all my cards on the table right now so you won't have any issues tomorrow night—and I trust you'll do the same. Agreed?"

Hawk nodded. "Continue."

"Garaar trusts me, evidenced by the fact that he asked me to provide security for the exchange."

Hawk's eyebrows rose slowly. "He freely told you about the exchange?"

"Not exactly. He told me that he had a business deal going down that could potentially give him some trouble. He asked me to make sure his place at the docks was locked down tight."

"Wait? He asked you to do that while another arm of his organization is trying to simultaneously kill you?"

"Yeah, lucky me, eh?" McGinn said before rescuing the eggs from the pan and sliding them onto a plate. He walked across the room and placed it on the table in front of Hawk.

"Seems a bit ham-fisted, don't you think?" Hawk asked.

McGinn nodded. "Al-Sabaab isn't the most organized bunch. I doubt Garaar has much contact with their leadership who would know about such an operation going on."

"Are you sure that Al-Shabaab was responsible for the attack on us at the compound?"

"I'd bet my life on it. Besides, we heard from other soldiers who said it was them. I'm confident that's who it was."

Alex mumbled something that was barely audible.

"What's that, princess?" McGinn asked, directing his comments toward Alex.

"I said it would've been nice to know all of this up front."

McGinn shrugged. "I'm sure it would have, but I didn't exactly have time to send you two my entire dossier before this operation went live. I figured we could just trust each other. Am I still right?"

Hawk nodded slowly. "At this point, what choice do we have?"

"Not exactly a strong affirmation there."

"This business is give and take. Right now, you're just asking me to give after you hid some very important information that is pertinent to this mission."

"Fine. You want to know everything? I'll tell it to you. I've been working on gaining Garaar's trust for several months now. I knew what he was up to with Al-Shabaab, and I knew the only way for him to trust me was for me to act as if I was a dirty CIA operative who could be bought."

Hawk tapped his finger against the side of his mug. He stared at McGinn for a few moments before responding. "Did you tell him that we were coming? Was that all part of gaining his trust?"

McGinn turned around and scooped the potatoes out of the pan before plating them. He took another sip of his coffee, lingering with his back to Hawk.

Hawk pounded his fist on the table. "Well, did you or not?"

McGinn sighed and turned around. "Sometimes you gotta do what you gotta do."

Alex stood up and walked across the room. "Not when it could get your partners killed."

"I knew they wouldn't kill you."

Hawk watched as Alex became fully awake—and angry.

"But what about all those other soldiers who were killed? What about those innocent people, too?" Alex asked.

McGinn slowly shook his head. "This is Somalia, Alex. There are no innocent people here."

"Maybe not, but they didn't deserve to die because you set them up. Was this really necessary?" she asked.

"To win his trust?" McGinn asked rhetorically. "Yes, it was. It was necessary because thousands of truly innocent people are going to die in America or Europe if those nut jobs at Al Hasib get ahold of the Sarin. I can promise you, nobody in the world will care about a bunch of militia men in training getting riddled with bullets. But if Sarin gas is unleashed in a populated area, the world will take note and strike back with a vengeance—and Al Hasib will have accomplished exactly what they wanted to: incite violence."

"This isn't a game," Hawk said.

"No, it's not," McGinn said. "There is a real possibility of Al Hasib getting their hands on this gas, and it can't happen. It's a serious threat, and it needs to be dealt with properly."

Hawk exhaled slowly. "You better know what you're doing with Garaar. Thousands of lives may be at stake, and Alex and I are willing to risk our lives to stop any potential threat. But your plan better not be giving us up, because I will hunt you down and kill you if I make it out alive."

McGinn held up his mug as if he were giving a mock toast.

"To trust," he said.

Hawk shot a glance at Alex. He could tell she wasn't buying McGinn's story either no matter how plausible it sounded.

CHAPTER 24

ARAV KATARI NAVIGATED *The Ajagar* through the Gulf of Aden and toward the Berbera harbor. He was still fifty kilometers away from his destination, which made him scan the horizon more closely for pirates. The closer he cruised toward the coast of Somalia, the greater the chance he would become a mark for the thieves roaming the sea.

The last time he was in this location, Katari knew he would get boarded. The elaborate deception he pulled that day was why he enjoyed a new car and air conditioning for the homes of everyone in his extended family. As he watched the pirates tear out across the water after removing several barrels of chemicals six months ago, his conscience started bothering him. It nagged him less as time wore on to the point where he'd convinced himself that his act could be construed as noble. Americans who were complicit in allowing their country's authoritarian view of capitalism would get what was coming to them. He was confident his family with more livable homes would agree. Though Katari still regretted killing Virk, yet it had to be done.

Katari scanned the horizon for any pirates. His hope that he would be able to slip into port without attracting any attention was met with disappointment. Picking up his binoculars to check, Katari realized the two boats he'd seen were headed straight toward them.

Aside from warning the crew with a brief announcement, there wasn't much else he could do to prepare for their looming encounter with the pirates. A few minutes later, the speed boats with machine gun mounts flanked Katari's ship. With guns trained on the *The Ajagar*, the smaller vessels made up for their lack of size with powerful weaponry, including a pair of handheld RPGs that had been welded to the front of the boats on swivels.

Katari stopped his ship. There was no need to drag on the inevitable. Besides, he didn't want anyone on the shore to see what was about to happen to the men who'd just made what would be a fatal mistake. A handful of crewmembers found their way to the deck to see why their ship had suddenly stopped moving. Katari wasn't sure which boat was in charge until one of the men aboard the starboard side vessel started speaking through a bullhorn.

"Attention, captain of *The Ajagar*, prepare to be boarded," the man said. "We intend to do you no harm."

Yeah, right, and I can pull an elephant around Mumbai on a rickshaw.

Katari smiled and waved, gesturing for the pirate captain to come aboard.

"Sir, you can't be serious," said Dalip, one of Katari's crewmembers.

"I am—very serious." Katari wagged his index finger. "You be sure to stay out of their way if you know what's best for you. Just let me do all the talking."

Moments later, the pirate's captain ascended the rope ladder that Katari had instructed his crew to drop down. The captain was followed by two other men who Katari labeled as fools.

Before the captain opened his mouth, Katari approached the man and stared sternly at him.

"I suggest you three climb back down that ladder and leave us alone," Katari said.

The captain broke into loud laughter. "Did you hear that? The good captain here wants us just to go home, perhaps pretend this whole thing never happened."

"That's not what I was—"

"Oh, sure it wasn't," the captain said as he

mocked Katari. "If I've boarded one ship out here in the gulf, I've boarded a thousand. They all try to convince me they have nothing to hide. But I always find what I'm looking for."

"And what do you plan on finding?"

"I think you know."

Katari growled, miffed that the pirates' ship captain was relentless and condescending. Katari was done listening. "Want to hear what I think of that?"

The captain stopped and glared at Katari. "Please enlighten us."

"Consider this your only warning. If you think you're just going to come aboard *my* ship and start taking my stuff, you're going to make a grave mistake."

The captain threw his head back and laughed. "Says the man without a gun." He turned serious and jammed the barrel of his rifle into Katari's stomach. "Now, if you know what's best for you, you'll sit down and keep your mouth shut."

"And if you know what's best for you, you'll leave now," Katari responded.

The captain used the butt of his rifle to knock Katari out.

When Katari regained consciousness a few minutes later, he watched the pirates handing loot down the ladder and into their boats. With his head still aching, he staggered to his feet. The captain pointed at Katari and laughed.

"Welcome back, but I suggest you stay down."

Katari bent over, resting his hands on his knees. He didn't look up to address the captain. "You were warned."

The captain laughed again before walking up to Katari and kicking him in the stomach. "Farewell, my friend."

Katari crumpled to the ground again and grabbed his midsection.

Dalip walked over and put his arm around Katari. "You still glad you did all the talking?"

"You still glad you stayed out of their way?" Katari shot back before grabbing his head.

"You talked tough, but those men just made off with some of our cargo. That won't sit well with your superiors."

"My superiors do not care about losing some worthless trinkets. They care about what I bring back."

Katari motioned for Dalip to follow him to the bridge, where Katari picked up a pair of binoculars. He scanned the horizon before hailing another ship on the radio. At the request of the man speaking on the other end, Katari gave him their current coordinates along with an estimate of the pirates' coordinates.

"Watch those two ships," Katari said as he handed the binoculars to Dalip.

After a minute, nothing happened other than the boats speeding farther away. Dalip put the binoculars down.

"What's the point of this?" Dalip asked.

"To show you that I am a man of my word. I warned that captain. Now he will pay."

Dalip resumed watching the pair of pirate ships on the horizon. As he was peering across the sea, he spotted a fiery explosion and then another.

"What the hell?" Dalip asked, slack jawed.

"We work for very powerful men," Katari said. "No one will get away with boarding us again."

"Certainly not those men."

"Indeed," Katari said with a slight chuckle. "But no one better cause us trouble on our return trip, especially any pirates."

"What are we supposed to pick up at port?" Dalip asked.

"Something very dangerous—something very dangerous to us all."

CHAPTER 25

RASHID QURESHI MENTALLY ran through his checklist while he finished his dinner. Everything was going according to the plan Fazil had laid out for him, everything except the issue of Brady Hawk. Qureshi relished the opportunity to take down the thorn in Al Hasib's side for the past year. Before Hawk entered the scene, Al Hasbi had operated unfettered throughout the Middle East. But that was no longer the case, costing Al Hasib money, resources, and well-trained operatives. Fazil's response to this aggressive stance wasn't to hide in caves like Osama Bin Laden had done. No, Fazil wanted to take the fight to the infidels on their turn, though it hadn't transpired as he hoped. That was a fact that Qureshi knew as painfully as anyone.

While Hawk had eliminated key Al Hasib personnel and disrupted weapon and resource streams, the attacks felt personal to Qureshi. When

Hawk killed Al Hasib's chief bombmaker Nasim Ghazi during a mission in Afghanistan, Qureshi was devasted. Ghazi was Qureshi's half-brother, and Qureshi vowed to avenge his death. If Qureshi brooded too long over the situation, he could become unhinged.

Qureshi's phone rang, rescuing him from spiraling out of control. He took a deep breath and answered the call. It was Fazil.

"Are you ready to complete the transaction tomorrow?" Fazil asked.

"Everything is in order," Qureshi said. "Garaar is jumpy, so I'm looking forward to wrapping this up and getting back."

"Keep Garaar focused, and don't let him do anything stupid. It should be an easy deal once we secure the product."

Qureshi stirred his after dinner tea. "Do you want me to deal with him as we previously discussed?"

"Nothing has changed," Fazil said, pausing briefly. "What about our other little issue?"

"Hawk?"

"Yes, how do you plan to apprehend him?"

"I have a plan, so no need to worry."

"You better bring him back alive."

"I will do my best," Qureshi said.

Qureshi hung up the phone and set it down on

the table. He hated lying to Fazil, but Qureshi figured he could ask for forgiveness later.

There was no way he was going to let Brady Hawk walk out of Somalia alive.

CHAPTER 26

Saturday
Tangier, Morocco

J.D. BLUNT SAT AT THE BAR and wrote out a list of places he thought he could hide. The number of countries that did not contain an extradition treaty with the U.S. wasn't exactly comprised of the world's hottest tourist destinations. Not that Blunt wanted to go on vacation, but he did have an acute desire to blend in to a culture where everyone was used to everyone else being strangers. If he went to virtually any of the nations on the list, he'd be sure to stand out. The only one that seemed palatable to him was the Marshall Islands. However, even that location was a tenuous choice since it had a treaty with the U.S. for protection, not to mention many dire predictions about how climate change was going to drown every inhabitant.

Blunt sighed and stared out at the Mediterranean

Sea, hoping that maybe a genius idea would fall out of the sky. It was a foolish thought, but he was desperate. He didn't want to face his new reality, one that meant the rest of his life would be spent on the lam.

His phone buzzed, jarring him back to reality. Christopher Roland's name appeared on the screen.

"Are you sure it's a good idea to be calling me?" Blunt asked.

"This will be my last call," Roland said, choosing his words carefully. "I simply wanted to make sure that your team was in place and that they were ready to begin the operation."

"As far as I know, it's a green light."

"Excellent. I will be in touch after they've completed their assignment."

Blunt hung up. He'd known Roland for a long time, but such friendship didn't equate to trust. If backed into a corner by the U.S. authorities or an international crime syndicate, Roland would give up Blunt. It wouldn't matter to Roland who was the consummate politician. No alliance was so sacred to Roland that it demanded his undying devotion.

Blunt signaled to the bartender to bring another glass of scotch. Fiddling with his phone, Blunt opened up the app he'd installed to check on his room. His paranoia had reached new heights. He realized his distrust of Roland was likely unwarranted given the long history of their friendship, but he'd been ambushed enough times that he quit giving anyone the benefit of the doubt many years ago. Blunt glanced at the screen and let out a low guttural sound.

He downed his drink then slammed the glass on the counter along. He slapped a twenty-dollar bill next to it and lumbered back toward his room. He looked at his phone again just to make sure he wasn't imagining things. He wasn't.

On Blunt's phone screen, the image of a man rummaging through his room was real. And it wasn't the hotel staff either. Blunt stomped upstairs and waited outside the door, which was slightly cracked. He could identify where the man was by peering into the room and looking at a mirror. The man's reflection was difficult to make out with any detail, but Blunt had no doubt the man wasn't supposed to be in there.

Blunt waited until the man walked behind the door. Then Blunt put his shoulder into the door, ramming it into the man's head and sending him sprawling. Blunt proceeded to deliver two quick punches followed by a stiff uppercut that knocked out the man. He searched for something to tie up the man with but found nothing. He hustled into the hallway and found an unattended cleaning cart. Checking to make sure no one could see, Blunt lifted several sets of sheets from the cart and carried them back to his room where he used the sheets to tie up the assailant.

Blunt then sat down at the small table in the kitchenette area and opened up the complimentary paper that had been shoved under his door earlier that morning. There was enough in English for him to read that would pre-occupy his time until the man regained consciousness.

While Blunt had plenty of questions, all Blunt could do was sit and wait.

CHAPTER 27

Berbera, Somalia

HAWK CLOSED ONE EYE and stared down the barrel with the other. It looked clear, but he brought it close to his mouth and blew a forceful breath through the barrel just to be sure. He pulled it away from his mouth, eyeing it once more.

"All clear," he announced, setting the gun on the table. He repeated the process several times with all the weapons he planned to strap to his body.

"A jam in the middle of a gunfight is a bitch," McGinn said. "Guys, I gotta tell you that I've got a good feeling about tonight."

Hawk set another gun on the table and glanced at McGinn before cutting his gaze over at Alex, who was looking at him. They both returned to their assignments, Hawk with the guns and Alex with the computers.

"That's good to hear," Alex said. "I'd hate for you to have a bad feeling before we entered battle together."

"I always have a good feeling," he said.

"As long as you have my back, we'll be okay," Hawk said, glancing up at McGinn.

"Of course I do," McGinn said. "Everything is going to run smoothly."

"I'll believe it when I see it," she said.

McGinn sighed and shook his head. "Don't be such a stick in the mud, Alex. To date, every mission I've ever been on, I've emerged without dying."

"There's always a first time," she said.

Hawk cracked a faint smile. If there was one thing he loved about Alex, it was that she was relentless. Even though they hadn't had much of an opportunity to fully discuss the fact that perhaps they were working with a man who'd been co-opted by the enemy, Hawk knew she understood the situation. They'd been working together long enough that words weren't always necessary. A look could sometimes say it all.

McGinn let out a long breath through his teeth He rolled his eyes at Alex's comment and continued prepping the explosives on the table.

"Are you always so optimistic, Alex?" McGinn asked.

She nodded. "It's what keeps me alive."

"Load up in five minutes," McGinn said, refusing to engage in any more witty banter.

Hawk collected every weapon he'd collected from his trip to McGinn's compound and headed for the SUV. Alex did likewise with all her computer equipment.

"Got any last-minute questions?" McGinn asked Alex as they walked out to the car.

Hawk turned around and watched Alex shake her head. It was obvious that his partner knew what she was doing and wasn't interested in giving McGinn any more inside information that might be detrimental to their ultimate objective: take possession of the Sarin gas.

"You need to be on your A game tonight," McGinn said. "One wrong move could cost all of us."

Alex scowled. "You think I don't already know that?"

"Just a reminder," he said.

Hawk stopped in front of the SUV and attempted to referee the argument taking place behind him.

"We need to get on the same page," Hawk said. "We're not going up against a fly-by-night operation here. Al Hasib and Al-Shabaab are two terrorists groups that know how to put everyone on edge. Please don't lose your edge by fighting amongst yourselves. We all need to be committed to working with and *for* one another. If you can't do that, then please sit this operation out."

Both Alex and McGinn looked somewhat sheepishly at Hawk.

"Thousands of people could die if we don't get our act together," Hawk said. "Now, let's get it together. Are you with me?"

Alex and McGinn both nodded and returned to their duties as they loaded up the SUV for surveillance.

McGinn tossed his last weapon into the trunk before slamming it shut.

"He isn't joking, you know?" McGinn said to Alex.

Alex watched Hawk walk back toward the building where there were plenty of other supplies, enough to make a two-day stand if necessary. To Hawk, every piece was important if they were going to survive the impending onslaught.

"If you have anything else, grab it now," McGinn said. "It's time to ride."

He turned the ignition and revved the gas, firing up the engine. "This won't be easy," he said with a smile.

Alex waved him off. "Nothing is ever easy."

Several minutes later, Hawk returned and

climbed into the passenger side front seat next to McGinn.

McGinn slapped the steering wheel and let out a yell of delight. "Hot damn," he said. "We're gonna kill us some terrorists tonight."

CHAPTER 28

GARAAR GLANCED AT his watch and continued to pace in the warehouse. He only stopped every minute or so when he drew near to the bank of closed-circuit security monitors on his desk. He hunched over and studied the image of each camera closely before moving on to the next one. The only activity he noticed was that of the Al-Shabaab guards patrolling the perimeter. Despite the fact that everything appeared quiet, Garaar remained worried.

At 10:50 p.m., Garaar decided to sit down after more than three hours of pacing and worrying. He opened up his Internet browser to see if he could find the latest message from Cindy. The message at the top of his inbox was a new one, denoted in a bold font. The combination of the email title along with the paper clip icon intrigued Garaar even more than usual when it came to Cindy's messages. The title read: Tasteful Party Boat Attire? Garaar clicked on the email with delight, knowing there wouldn't be anything tasteful about it. A grin slowly spread across Garaar's face as he stared at the buxom blonde.

Cindy's attire barely qualified as clothing and, Garaar deduced, would not likely withstand the mild rigors of a fifty-meter lap swim.

But perhaps that is the point.

Garaar gawked at the picture of Cindy for a couple minutes before he crafted a response to her picture, which didn't include any message.

That is most tasteful, Cindy. I hope you plan on wearing that when you come visit me at my yacht next week. Can't wait.

When Garaar pressed the send button, he glanced up at the time in the corner of the screen. He had less three minutes before the buyer was scheduled to arrive. Checking the monitors once again, he noticed someone had arrived. He enlarged the camera to fill the entire screen, studying the faces of the men in the picture slowly. The exchange was supposed to be between him and two men representing Al Hasib. But there were six men at the door with one of his guards.

"I don't like this," Garaar said aloud.

One of the security guards he'd hired had been standing in the room for several minutes, silent.

"What don't you like?" the guard asked.

Garaar jumped before he spun around to look in

the direction of the voice coming from the other side of the room.

"Don't you ever scare me like that again," Garaar said as he shook a finger at the guard.

"I thought you had seen me," the guard replied.

Garaar stood up. "Just go get three other guards and bring them in here. I don't like being so outnumbered."

"There is only one other guard in the building. The rest are patrolling the perimeter and need to remain outside."

"I don't care. Call them off their post," Garaar said.

"But I don't think that's—"

"I don't care what you think. We have other help regarding the security of the facility that you don't even know about. Go get three other guards, and bring them in here."

The guard broke into a slow jog as he left the room.

Garaar watched him leave and then exhaled a long breath. He then wrung his hands as he struggled to gather his wits.

"Okay, okay," he said aloud to himself. "This is simple. I've done this before. Just set up the demonstration, and it'll be fine."

He walked over to the sealed room where he

performed the tests and made sure the guinea pig was still awake and ready. After that, he rushed back into his office and cued up the video he'd previously sent to Karif Fazil to gauge his interest. But Garaar figured it would make for a more convincing presentation.

After a few moments, the guard returned with three other men.

"We're here, sir," the guard said.

"Good," Garaar said. "They'll be here any mo—"

The main door swung open, cutting off Garaar.

"Sir, are these the men you were expecting?" the lone guard accompanying the visitors said.

Garaar nodded.

"If you have nothing else for me, I will return to my post out front," the guard said.

"No, you can stay," Garaar said as he walked over to meet his guests. He swallowed hard as he studied the men and their weapons.

"Are those really necessary, Rashid?" Garaar asked, gesturing toward the guns.

Rashid Qureshi smiled. "Not for you, my friend." He motioned for his men to point their guns down. "Now, let's get down to business, shall we?"

Garaar nodded and pointed toward a projection screen descending slowly from the ceiling.

"We came here for a product, not a movie," Qureshi said.

Garaar shrugged. "I know. I just thought that—"

"Just give us a demonstration on one of your little animals, and we'll call it good," Qureshi said. "I don't want to stay around here long."

Garaar smiled. "You have nothing to worry about. There are men stationed outside who are the best of the best when it comes to security."

"That's what I'm afraid of," Qureshi said as he snapped his fingers. "Let's get on with it."

"Fine," Garaar said as he wrung his hands again. "Follow me."

Garaar led Qureshi and his entourage to the sealed room before opening the case containing the Sarin liquid. Donning a mask and gloves, Garaar carefully placed a few drops of liquid into a vaporizer.

"Make sure when you handle this that you always wear proper equipment," Garaar said, glancing at Qureshi to make sure he was paying attention.

Garaar slipped inside the room and placed the vaporizer into one of the hands of the glove box. He shut the door behind him and pressed a button, sealing the room.

"Do we need to wear masks?" Qureshi asked as he shifted his weight between his feet. "If anything went wrong ..."

"This is a small amount of gas," Garaar said. "It would mess you up, but it wouldn't kill you. This guinea pig, on the other hand, is going to die quickly."

Garaar turned around to face the room before he slid his hands into the openings in the box. He proceeded to vaporize the Sarin and took a step back to watch the small little animal twitch and turn until it was dead. The whole process took less than forty-five seconds.

"Impressive," Qureshi said. "It is just as you said. I'll take it." He held his hand open, palm up to Garaar.

Garaar held up his index finger. "Not until I get confirmation that you have sent the money to my account."

Qureshi rolled his eyes. "You scientists can be so finicky."

Garaar sighed and looked upward. "I'm first a jihadist before I'm a scientist—just like you."

"We're nothing alike," Qureshi said. He snapped then pointed at one of the men in his party who was clutching a laptop. "Make it happen."

The man opened his computer and started typing on the keyboard. "Can you provide me with the account number?" he asked Garaar.

Garaar grinned and placed a business card with his account number scrawled across it along with some other pertinent personal information that could help the bank identify him. "That should be all you need."

Qureshi laughed. "It sure is," he said.

Then he pulled out his gun and shot all the guards in formulaic fashion before training it on Garaar. Slack-jawed, Garaar watched all the men supposedly protecting him crumple to the ground.

"There isn't going to be a transfer of funds tonight," Qureshi said. "But I am going to test out the Sarin on you."

Garaar looked up at Qureshi in horror. "You can't—you wouldn't," Garaar stammered.

"You're right. I won't," Qureshi said right before he peppered Garaar with four shots.

CHAPTER 29

HAWK REPELLED DOWN to the ground floor through an opening in the skylight. No more than twenty meters away, McGinn was a mirror image of Hawk. When Hawk's feet hit the floor, he flicked his rope, creating some slack before he yanked it down. As he rolled up the rope, he crept across the room and hid behind a set of cabinets.

"You read me, Wonder Woman?" Hawk said.

"Wonder Woman? I'm flattered. Is that how you see me, Hawk?" Alex asked.

"If you help us get out of this alive, I will."

McGinn, who'd also released his rope, waved vigorously, motioning for Hawk to be quiet.

Hawk gave him a thumbs up sign.

"What's our situation now?" Hawk asked in a whisper.

"Well, you won't have to worry about Garaar," Alex answered. "The Al Hasib team just gunned him down. But keep your head on a swivel because they're headed your way."

"Roger that."

Hawk fixed his gaze on the doors closest to him where the terrorists would likely enter the room. McGinn had selected this room to stage an ambush because it could serve as a kill box, a small enclosed area where the initiating party held the tactical advantage. In this case, Hawk and Alex had the element of surprise to go on their side along with the best position in the room from which to eliminate the Al Hasib operatives.

While he waited, Hawk wondered if there wasn't a better way to seize the Sarin. With all the advanced information McGinn possessed, Hawk still wondered why they didn't simply bar the doors from the outside and drop in some gas to immobilize the Al Hasib team. Taking possession of the gas, not to mention the elimination of the agents, would've been cleaner and simpler. But McGinn insisted the Al Hasib agents would have gas masks and be prepared for such an ambush. Instead, McGinn's plan felt to Hawk as if it were the most dangerous one of all. McGinn's attempted to assuage Hawk's fears by explaining how they were going to take out some of Al Hasib's best agents as well as eliminate Al-Shabaab's chemical weapons expert.

So far, McGinn was at least right about Garaar, even if they didn't have to pull the trigger to kill him.

"If the feed I hacked and am looking at is accurate, they should be there within the next five seconds," Alex said, her voice crackling over the com links.

"Is there any reason it wouldn't be accurate?" Hawk asked.

Before Alex could answer, Hawk watched the doorknob turn slowly and a handful of men storm in. Immediately, Hawk could tell they were the Al Hasib agents he'd seen from the security cameras that Alex had hacked within minutes of arriving on location.

As the door swung open, McGinn unleashed a flurry of bullets on the Al Hasib agents. Hawk had told McGinn to wait until the men were boxed in between them and had no opportunity to escape without walking through the line of fire.

Screw it.

Hawk joined McGinn in riddling the men with bullets, an ambush that initially appeared to be a rousing success. A faint grin spread across Hawk's face as two, three, then four operatives collapsed to the ground. Loud moans filled the room as the men grappled with the reality of their situation. Hawk inspected the agents, searching for the case of chemical weapons.

"Do you see the Sarin?" McGinn called from across the room.

Hawk turned the lights on and began removing weapons from the dying men's hands. One man writhing in pain begged Hawk to shoot him, and Hawk obliged. But still no weapons case.

"You find it yet?" McGinn asked as he made his way toward the bodies.

"There were six men in the image Alex showed us, right?" Hawk asked.

"Roger that," Alex said. "I'm looking at it again right now. And I only see four bodies on the feed I'm looking at. Are two outside the camera's field?"

"You can see everything we can," McGinn answered back.

"Well, there are two more men running around here somewhere. Let me see if I can pinpoint their location for you," Alex said.

"Ah-ha! Found it," Hawk said, using his foot to roll over one of the men, who'd fallen on top of the chemical weapons case.

McGinn knelt down and opened the case. He quickly shut it and picked it up. "This is it."

Hawk stared down at the bodies strewn around the room and pumped his fist. "Now we just need to track down those other two agents to make this a clean sweep."

Then he felt the cold barrel of a gun against the back of his neck.

"Don't move another muscle or you're dead," McGinn said.

Hawk laid his weapon on the ground and raised his hands in surrender. "Unbelievable," Hawk said. "I thought I could trust you."

"You still can," McGinn said. "You're still alive, aren't you?"

Hawk narrowed his eyes and turned to glare at McGinn. "So, what are you waiting on?"

"I made a deal," McGinn said, keeping his gun trained on Hawk while securing the door through which the operatives had entered. "I deliver you to Al Hasib, I make off with the Sarin."

Hawk shook his head. "And they're just going to let you walk away with their weapon? I hardly think that's going to happen."

McGinn collected all the weapons off the men and then walked briskly to the other side of the room. He opened the door, keeping it ajar with his foot so he could address Hawk before exiting.

"Think whatever you wish, but I happen to know where the bigger cache of Sarin is—and that's where the other agents are headed. But only after they tie up some loose ends with you."

"Loose ends?" Hawk asked.

"Goodbye, Hawk. It's been a pleasure knowing you. No hard feelings. Just a good business decision on my end."

"You better hope they kill me," Hawk said with a growl.

"Oh, they will. The man coming for you is the stepbrother of a man you recently killed. Good luck."

McGinn slammed the door shut. Hawk could hear what sounded like a metal chain being wrapped around the double doors. He rushed over to them, shaking the handles. They barely budged.

Hawk wanted to hit something, preferably John McGinn, but needed to gather his wits if he was going to survive. Then, he heard a voice over his comlink that made him cringe.

"Mr. Hawk, I believe I've got something that belongs to you. Or should I say *someone*?" said a man.

"Who is this?"

"Oh, Mr. Hawk, you don't know me, but you ran into my stepbrother once—and you killed him. Does the name Nasim Ghazi sound familiar?"

Hawk knew the name all too well, but he didn't want to give the caller any more reason to hate him. "You're going to have to help me out. I'm drawing a blank."

"You disgust me," Qureshi said. "You insult the memory of my brother, a man you needlessly killed."

"I'm going to kill you!" Hawk said.

Qureshi broke into a hearty laugh. "You're going to kill me? That just might be one of the funniest things I've heard in months. But I'm a fair man, so I'm willing to give you a fighting chance. You have ten minutes to find me. After ten minutes, I'm going to kill your little friend Alex. Or maybe I have other plans for her before I kill her. You'll never know if you don't arrive in time. I'll be waiting—and watching."

In the background, Hawk heard Alex yell.

"Don't do it, Hawk. Just leave me. Get out of there and grab the weapon."

Then a high-pitched shriek followed by another scream.

"Ten minutes," Qureshi said before the com went silent.

CHAPTER 30

McGINN TUGGED ON THE CHAIN he wrapped around the handles to make sure the doors were secure. Satisfied with his work, he shoved an extra gun he'd lifted off the Al Hasib agents into the back of his pants, picked up the weapon and his gun, and headed toward the dock.

Once he exited the building, he raced down a set of stairs toward the port where he'd arranged to meet his contact. But he was nowhere to be found.

What the hell? Where is he?

While mildly annoyed, McGinn wasn't concerned. He'd just locked Brady Hawk up in a kill box, though McGinn all but assured he'd never see the Firestorm assassin again after giving away Alex's position. It was a plan he'd managed to execute flawlessly. All Qureshi had to do was finish off Hawk and Alex, which wouldn't be difficult given their situations.

McGinn dialed a number on his cell phone, but the call went straight to voicemail.

Crouching behind a shipping container, McGinn could only wait and think. He actually thought Hawk was a good man, but McGinn was just following orders, like a good soldier does, even if he didn't understand why or agree with the reason given. McGinn thought the order seemed harsh, particularly since Hawk had eliminated some of the CIA's top threats globally in recent months. But McGinn operated in a black-and-white world: orders were orders. Who was he to challenge such a directive?

McGinn peered around the edge of the container toward the water. He saw what looked like a faint glimmer in the distance. The ship was heading straight toward the dock.

It was only a matter of minutes before he could vanish and never to set foot in Somalia again.

And it couldn't happen quickly enough for McGinn's liking.

CHAPTER 31

HAWK RUSHED TOWARD the other door, rattling it with both hands. But it didn't budge. He then grabbed the rope he'd repelled into the room on and tried to search for a place to secure it and climb up and out. In the operation planning, he suggested to McGinn that they should have an alternative way out in case things went sideways, but McGinn nixed the idea, claiming that it would also create a way for more assailants to access the room and potentially entrap them.

That dirty backstabbing bastard. This was a set up from the beginning.

Hawk blamed himself for not seeing it, then blamed Blunt for being too trusting with one of his old friends from Congress. But then Hawk stopped. He needed to expend his mental energy on figuring out a way to escape the room.

Once more, Hawk surveyed his surroundings.

The room appeared to be a storage area without much in the way of storage. It was mostly open with the exception of a few shelving units with a scant number of supplies. The double doors at each end of the room were secured, and the only other portals were the skylights above. No windows to jump through.

For a moment, Hawk even contemplated putting a hole in the wall until he realized thick aluminum comprised all four sides. He looked over the supplies but couldn't find anything of use. A few beakers, a microscope, some dyes, stacks of washcloths, petri dishes.

If I wanted to make some hippy tie-dye headbands, I'd be in heaven right now.

But he wasn't. He was in a hell of McGinn's making. McGinn hadn't just met with Garaar—they plotted together.

Hawk noticed a blinking red light in the corner on the side of the security camera. There was another camera on the other side of the room as well. Without a clear way out, Hawk decided he wasn't going to give Qureshi the pleasure of seeing him struggle. Hawk hung washcloths over the camera lenses and plotted his next move.

Hawk's com link crackled to life with Qureshi on the other end.

"You might think you are clever by covering the

cameras, but your little friend is going to die in five minutes if you don't meet me in the lab," Qureshi said. "I know you know where it's at since I found the schematics of the building with your friend here. Five minutes. Not a second more."

Hawk seethed. "I swear I'll kill you when I find you."

"All your empty threats won't save your friend's life. Better hurry."

The line went silent. Hawk shook his head as he looked around the room. He'd spent five minutes trying to figure a way out, and he was convinced this was exactly the plan that McGinn had conceived and hatched with Qureshi.

Of all the times to be in this situation … *and Alex is gonna die.*

Hawk interlocked his fingers and put his hands on his head.

He was definitely in a kill box, but it wasn't him who was going to die, at least not first.

CHAPTER 32

ARAV KATARI NAVIGATED *The Ajagar* into the port and eased it against the docking station. His crew worked quickly to secure the vessel, while he watched from ground. Directions were shouted back and forth. Ropes were tied off. Crewmembers scurried across the deck.

"I hope they can reverse what they've done just as quickly," said a man.

Katari turned around to see John McGinn standing a few feet away.

"They make lightning seem slow," Katari said, offering his hand to McGinn.

McGinn smiled as he shook Katari's hand. "Let's get out of here so we can avoid any potential trouble."

"Trouble?"

"I don't want to press my luck," McGinn said. "I just left an assassin locked up, but I'm not inclined to hang around to see if he somehow managed to survive."

"An assassin?"

McGinn waved dismissively at Katari. "Let's just get going."

Katari nodded. "Do you have the promised amount?"

"Two hundred and fifty thousand U.S. dollars?" McGinn asked.

"I was told it would be a half million."

McGinn sighed. "That's more than I was told to deliver."

"I'm not going anywhere until I have the money in my account."

"You get nothing if you don't get this ship out of the harbor and quickly."

Katari eyed McGinn closely. "Two hundred fifty now and two hundred fifty when we arrive. I won't let you off until I receive the amount promised to me in full."

"Fine," McGinn said. "I'll see what I can do."

"No, you'll do it or you won't leave this ship," Katari said, snatching the case from McGinn's hands. "And I'll take this as insurance."

"Be careful with that," McGinn said. "I'll make sure you get what you were promised. Just get us the hell out of here, okay?"

"I'm supposed to pick up another man."

"Whoever he is, I know he's not promising you

the kind of cash you'll be getting from me. Let's go. Now."

Katari nodded and whistled at his crew, gesturing at them. They knew what it meant. They needed to prepare to leave the harbor.

CHAPTER 33

HAWK GLANCED AT HIS WATCH and let out a long breath. Only four minutes remained before Qureshi would make good on his promise and kill Alex. The situation wasn't a promising one as Hawk had run out of options.

As he looked around the room yet again in search of something that could help him escape, he heard a smack on the concrete floor. He turned around to see a rope dangling from the skylight and reaching all the way to the ground.

"Well, don't just stand there and gawk. Get a move on," said the person hunched over the skylight.

It was Emily.

Hawk shimmied up the rope in less than a minute.

"I thought I told you not to contact me again," he said as he reached the roof.

"A thank you might be more in order," Emily shot back.

Hawk ignored her. "We've got to get to the lab. Some Al Hasib agent is going to kill Alex if I don't get to her in the next couple minutes."

"And what? So he can kill you instead? I don't think you've thought this through."

"Look, if I don't make it out for some reason, I want you to take care of Alex and make sure she gets home safe."

"I'm coming with you," she said.

"No, you can't. They'll shoot her on site. I can't have that. I need to do this my way."

Emily bit her bottom lip before speaking. "Fine. Do it your way. I'll be watching though in case things go sideways."

"Wish me luck," Hawk said before he slid down the roof, jumped to a pole, and shimmied down to the ground.

He sprinted toward the lab and then stopped in front. Taking a deep breath, he turned the knob and entered the room, both hands raised in the air.

"What are you doing, Hawk?" Alex asked.

Hawk locked eyes with her and remained solemn, walking slowly toward who he assumed was Qureshi.

"You have me now," Hawk said. "You can let her go."

Qureshi laughed. "You thought I was actually going to let her go? Oh, you Americans are so naïve."

He shoved Alex toward the lone guard flanking him. "Take care of her."

"Be a man of your word," Hawk said, still moving slowly toward Qureshi. "We both know you don't care about her. It's me you want."

"You might be right, but that's not going to change my mind. However, I'll let Ahmad have a little fun with her before he finishes her off. But you are all mine."

Hawk had walked close enough that he was in striking distance. Unexpectedly to Qureshi, Hawk ducked down and kicked at Qureshi's knee cap, crippling him. Qureshi yelped in agony and instinctively reached down to grab his knee. Hawk proceeded to seize the opportunity, delivering a vicious blow to Qureshi's neck.

As Qureshi tumbled toward the ground, Hawk grabbed Qureshi's hand that held his gun and pointed it at his guard, squeezing off two shots, one of which hit his guard in the head. Qureshi struggled to pull away from Hawk as the two men fell to the ground, tussling over the weapon still in Qureshi's hand.

Hawk delivered a combination of powerful uppercuts to Qureshi's body and then to his face. But Qureshi fought back, stomping on Hawk's knee to send him to the ground. However, Hawk didn't relinquish his grip on the gun.

Qureshi jerked his hand to the left and then rapidly

to the right, utilizing Hawk's leverage to point the gun at Alex. Qureshi then squeezed off a shot, hitting Alex. She stumbled backward and fell to the ground.

Enraged, Hawk kicked Qureshi in the stomach and proceeded to rip the gun away from him.

Hawk fired two bullets into Qureshi's companion, the fellow Al Hasib agent.

Qureshi staggered for a few seconds before falling to the ground.

"When I killed your brother, it wasn't personal," Hawk said. "But I promised you that you would die. I always keep my word."

Hawk didn't hesitate, shooting Qureshi twice, once in the head, another time in the chest. After Hawk was sure Qureshi was dead, Hawk rushed over to Alex.

"Are you okay?" he asked as he knelt down next to her.

"I think I'll live. It's just a flesh wound."

Hawk smiled and ripped a section of Qureshi's shirt off, using it as a bandage to tie around Alex's arm.

"Are you sure you're okay?" he asked again.

"Stop fussing over me," she said. "We need to get that weapon back from McGinn."

"Yeah, you're fine," Hawk said.

"I know. Let's get moving. We don't have any time to waste."

CHAPTER 34

ARAV KATARI STRAINED TO SEE into the dimly lit dock for a person running toward his ship. He'd promised to wait for an Al Hasib agent even though Katari had never seen the man. Katari agreed to split the twenty-thousand dollars the man had promised with three other crewmembers. When an opportunity like that came along, Katari refused to pass it up. He knew how hard his crew worked, and he knew who could keep a secret.

He was still scanning the docks when he felt sharp cold steel pressed against his neck. Katari glanced down at the knife and froze.

"It's time to go," McGinn said. "I'm not paying you to be a taxi service. Whoever you're waiting on isn't coming."

Katari turned around slowly. "And neither is whoever you're afraid of. There hasn't been any movement along the docks in at least ten minutes."

"All the more reason to leave now and stop

wasting my time."

Katari raised both his hands in a gesture of surrender and strode toward the ship's bridge.

"Faster," McGinn growled. "I've got people to meet."

Picking up his pace, Katari skipped steps as he climbed the stairs leading to the bridge. He picked up his radio and gave the order for the ship to be released from the dock. Katari watched as the crewmembers hustled back and forth to get the ship in position to push back out to sea.

McGinn, who'd followed, had put his knife away in favor of a gun.

"Who are you so scared of?" Katari asked, nodding toward McGinn's weapon. "No one is going to attack you aboard my ship."

"It's not anyone on your ship I'm worried about."

"Well, you can put that thing away now. We just cleared the dock, and we're almost fully in the channel. I can guarantee you that we don't have any stowaways."

McGinn remained stoic, vigilant in his self-appointed lookout position.

"You can relax, Mr. McGinn," Katari said. "Go enjoy yourself in the galley. Drink a beer."

After a few more moments of silence, McGinn exhaled and a wry grin spread across his fan. "You're probably right. That bastard couldn't follow us this far."

CHAPTER 35

HAWK AND ALEX DIDN'T SO MUCH move as they heard footsteps approaching. Lying flat on their backs in one of the ship's lifeboats, they both held their breath and waited for the men patrolling the deck to pass. Once their voices faded, Hawk let out a long breath as did Alex.

"So we made it on board," Alex said. "Now what?"

"You need to stay put while I go deal with McGinn."

"Oh, come on, Hawk. You're just gonna leave me here to twist in the wind. At least give me a weapon to defend myself."

Hawk eyed her closely. "If you stay here, you shouldn't need a weapon. I don't plan on capsizing the ship, but if I do, you're in the best place to be. Just release that lever on top and …"

"If this boat starts to sink, I'm certain I'll have

company. I'm not sure the guys on board are the women-and-children-first type of sailors."

Reluctantly, Hawk handed her the extra weapon he'd picked up. "Whatever you do, don't leave this lifeboat. I'll be back shortly."

Hawk peeked out from beneath the tarp to make sure no one could see him. Once he was convinced the coast was clear, he slipped onto the deck and steadied the boat before sneaking down into the hull of the ship. Tugging his hat down low across his face, Hawk moved through the ship as if he were almost invisible. He'd observed how disjointed the crewmembers seemed to be and how they rarely used each other's names while communicating, particularly the captain. It was a patchwork crew, and Hawk acted on his suspicion that they wouldn't even know if he was part of the crew. And he was right.

Hawk's search throughout the ship for McGinn wasn't an easy one. Twice he thought he spotted McGinn, but the traitor wouldn't stop moving. In one hand, he was clutching the weapon; in the other, a gun. Hawk quickly realized he would have to make this kill in tight quarters. A gunfight would put Hawk in a precarious situation with the rest of the crew, and he only had one clip.

After a few minutes of trailing McGinn, Hawk saw an opportunity to make his move when McGinn entered the boiler room. Hustling to catch up, Hawk crept inside and crouched low. McGinn's footsteps echoed off the walls, the metallic reverb creating a gracious cover for Hawk to move into place.

"I know you're in here," McGinn said. "I spotted you a couple minutes ago. But I wanted you in here. Apparently, I need to finish the job that Qureshi couldn't finish."

Hawk wanted to tell McGinn that Qureshi was dead, but Hawk refused to give away his position on a vain retort.

"Don't worry," McGinn said. "I know where you are, and I'm going to end this right now."

The room wasn't well lit, relying on a handful of lights encased in red glass against the wall to illuminate what was visible. Hawk remained low to the ground, moving stealthily into position to surprise McGinn.

Peeking around one of the pistons, Hawk made eye contact with McGinn, who didn't hesitate to fire a shot in Hawk's direction. With two doors on opposite sides of the room, he realized he'd walked into another kill box. But without another couple of soldiers, it wouldn't serve as one for him.

Then Hawk heard footsteps storming toward the boiler room. He braced for the showdown.

CHAPTER 36

ALEX ONLY MOVED TO BLINK and breathe as she lay on her back staring up at the tarp covering the lifeboat. The chatter on the deck was sporadic and calm, likely the opposite of what was occurring below if Hawk had ventured there in pursuit of McGinn. After ten minutes, she decided that it was a waste for her to remain pat. Getting the Sarin was one thing; turning the ship around to head back to port was another. But the latter was something she could influence the captain to do.

She waited until the footsteps of the patrolling guards faded before peeking through the tarp to inspect the deck. It was clear. As she wrestled with the tie downs, Alex feared she might make too much noise and attract attention. She finally jiggled the rope free and lifted the tarp. Taking great paints to ensure a silent exit, Alex slid through the opening she'd created by loosening the covering and climbed onto the deck.

It was a nearly flawless exit until the boat started to sway, the hinges squeaking loudly.

She ducked behind a couple nearby crates in the hopes that no one would spot her. Alex peeked around the side but didn't notice anybody. She remained crouched low as she scampered across the deck to the base of the steps leading to the ship's bridge. Standing with her back flushed against the wall, she took a deep breath.

There's a reason why I'm not fond of field work.

After checking both directions, she stepped away from the wall and was about to walk up the steps when she heard a man speak from behind her.

"Not another move," he said.

Alex put her hands in the air and turned around to see a guard with his rifle trained on her. He motioned for her to walk back down the steps.

"Place your gun on the ground," he said.

She complied, kneeling slowly to lay her gun down. While she did this, she scanned the area for anything that might help her gain an advantage on the guard. Out of the corner of her eye, she spotted a fire extinguisher attached to the wall. Slowly rising to an upright position, she eyed the man closely.

"Is there a problem?" she asked, flipping her hair back.

The guard seemed taken aback by the slight

flirtatious act, his eyes diverting down for a second. And that was all the time Alex needed.

She ripped the fire extinguisher out of its holder and swung it at the guard's head. The blow sent him stumbling backward across the deck toward the edge. Alex ran after him and delivered another devastating hit, knocking the man out cold.

After tossing the extinguisher into the water, Alex proceeded to strip the man of all weapons he carried, including a tactical knife and two hand guns. She threw his rifle into the water for good measure.

With the guard out, she dragged him to a storage room off the main deck and shut him up inside. The deck remained quiet, yet she maintained her low profile, sneaking across the deck and climbing up the steps to the bridge. She slipped inside and caught the captain off guard.

"What's going on here?" asked the captain, scowling at Alex.

"You're going to take us back to Berbera right now," she said.

"I don't think so."

"Me and my gun say otherwise."

"Look, I don't know who you are, but you can't hijack my boat like this," he said. "There will be people up here soon, and you will be outnumbered."

"Perhaps I'll just shoot you and turn the ship

206 | R.J. PATTERSON

around myself."

The captain laughed. "Let's be honest. You're not going to use that thing."

Alex fired a shot at the captain's foot, ripping a hole in it.

The captain hopped around on one foot, screaming in pain.

"Let's go over this once more slowly," she said. "You need to turn this ship around right now and take us back to Berbera."

The captain knelt and grabbed his foot, writhing for a few moments in pain before he staggered to his feet. He spun the wheel around as the ship slowly began to backtrack over its previous course.

"Maybe next time you'll do what I say the first time I ask," Alex said.

CHAPTER 37

THE SHIP LURCHED PORTSIDE and groaned as she turned. Outside the doorway to the boiler room, Hawk heard a clatter of footfalls and retreated, standing flush against the wall. The last thing he wanted was for the crew members to open the door to the room and see him first they after entering the room.

When the door flung open seconds later, two men hustled downstairs, stopping two steps shy of the bottom. They both wildly waved their guns into the dimly lit room.

"Where is he?" one of the guards asked.

"Look to your right," McGinn said.

Hawk's head was flush against the walls as he looked left at the doorway. He had less than half a second to decide what to do as the crew members would inevitably whip their heads in his direction.

Thinking quickly, Hawk fired a shot at one of the

pipes on the other side of the room, throwing the men into confusion. Instead of looking right like McGinn had said, they turned left and shot blindly toward some electrical equipment. Sparks flew, and McGinn screamed at the men to stop. But it was too late. Hawk had stealthily climbed onto the steps behind them. With such precision and efficiency, he stabbed both of the men in the back of the neck. It happened so quickly that the man on the right had started to collapse to the floor before the man on the left even noticed what was happening. Neither ever had a fighting chance.

Hawk used the handrail to swing back down to the ground floor. He worked his way around the room while McGinn blabbered away, giving away his precise location each time.

"If you're lucky enough to kill me, Hawk, just know that this endless parade of betrayal and attacks are never going to stop," McGinn said. "You're on the CIA's most wanted list now."

Tell me something I don't already know.

Hawk felt the door behind him on the far side of the room from where he had entered. He needed to flush McGinn out into the open to get a clean shot.

"President Michaels knows about Firestorm now, too," McGinn said again. "It's over. You're done. The whole project is going to be shuddered, especially after you screwed things up in Washington."

Hawk tried to ignore McGinn, who apparently knew quite a few more details about Hawk than he would've guessed. All it did was make Hawk angrier.

I'm gonna take you bastards out one at a time then.

Hawk continued with this dance around the room until a pattern emerged from McGinn's movements. Even as random as McGinn had to think he was being, Hawk had figured out McGinn's next move and was one step ahead of him.

Hawk moved into position and waited, enduring more drivel from McGinn in the process.

"You, Alex, Blunt—you're all gonna die," McGinn said.

Hawk exploded from his position, delivering a swift punch to McGinn's throat. McGinn staggered back and attempted to raise his weapon and get off a shot at Hawk. But Hawk kicked the gun out of McGinn's hand before bull rushing him. Hawk placed his shoulder into the center of McGinn's sternum and drove him against the wall. The thud of McGinn's back hitting the steel beam was followed by a crack. Hawk unleashed a wicked punch to McGinn's nose, breaking it and sending McGinn to the ground.

But before McGinn slunk all the way to the floor, Hawk ripped free the knife that McGinn had tucked into the side of his belt.

"In case you haven't noticed, I'm not a big fan of terrorism, no matter who is doing the terrorizing," Hawk said. "But I trust myself more than anyone else, and I know what's going on here."

"And what is that exactly?" McGinn asked.

"You sabotaged this mission to get rich," Hawk said.

McGinn laughed and shook his head. "You think you know me so well, do you? I hate to break it to you, Hawk, but that's not the kind of man I am."

"You certainly aren't a man of principal."

"No, I'm much more—I'm a man of duty. And that's exactly what I was doing here. I was fulfilling my duty."

"To steal Sarin for the CIA."

McGinn sneered. "If you only knew."

"Enlighten me."

"I don't care to waste my last few breaths."

Hawk knelt so he could look McGinn in the eyes. "You set me and Alex up. I could pardon you for trying to kill me. But Alex?"

"Just get it over with," McGinn said as he lunged for the knife in Hawk's hand.

Hawk yanked the knife back in an attempt to move it out of McGinn's reach.

"You bastard. Don't drag this out," McGinn snapped.

Hawk grabbed McGinn's ear and pulled his head to the side before inserting the knife into his chest. "Whatever horrors my own government planned end today."

McGinn slumped down, his eyes barely open, life fleeting from his body. "They will find you, you know."

Hawk wiped the bloody blade off on his pants. "I'm counting on it."

CHAPTER 38

AN HOUR LATER, *The Ajagar* entered the harbor in Berbera with a frazzled Captain Katari at the helm. Hawk stood calmly behind the captain. Other than revenge, there was no reason for Katari to retaliate against Hawk and Alex. The package that McGinn had entrusted Katari to transport had been dumped into the Arabian Sea, and, with it, Katari's big payday.

"I know it may feel like a disappointment now," Hawk began, "but you would've lived with a lifetime of regret the moment you heard about the hundreds of people killed by Sarin gas. Trust me. We did you a favor."

Katari didn't flinch, keeping his eyes on the waterway in front of his ship.

"McGinn would've probably killed you anyway," Alex said. "Had you even seen any money."

Katari wouldn't turn around.

Hawk fingered the gun in his pocket, unsure if

Katari might explode. "I hope you understand this isn't personal for us, but we were sent here to do a job. Somewhere along the way, we were ambushed, yet we never wavered in our mission. I'm sure as a captain you can appreciate that."

Nodding almost indiscernibly, Katari continued steering the ship to the port they'd departed from a few hours before.

They continued on for a few minutes in silence before Katari spoke.

"Do you know what it's like to see your family suffer? To watch your grandmother nearly faint due to the unbearable heat? To listen to the cries of your son with a hungry belly? I take no pride in what I did, but I saw an opportunity to change the course of my family's life, to give them a chance to thrive instead of survive. And I did what any man would do—I took it."

"But is that worth your integrity?" Hawk asked.

"Integrity doesn't keep our homes cool or put food on the table. But money does," Katari said, shaking his fist.

"If it's blood money, the cost is always too high."

Katari didn't say a word, seething until the ship docked.

"Give me your account number, and I'll see that you're compensated from a source that will reward you for doing the right thing," Hawk said.

Katari exhaled and shrugged. "What can it hurt?"

"It will ease the pain," Hawk said. "I understand your predicament, but I cannot allow such injustice to become the way my own country operates, even if this mission eventually costs me my life. I will not see innocent blood spilled."

Katari scratched out a string of numbers on a scrap piece of paper and held it out to Hawk. "Don't let me down."

Hawk looked Katari in the eyes as he took the paper. "I won't. You have my word."

Hawk and Alex departed the ship and watched as it churned back out into the channel.

"So you're going to deposit a large sum of money into the captain's banking account?" she asked.

Hawk maintained his gaze across the water and nodded. "I'm sure Blunt can find enough money underneath his couch cushions to pay this." He held out the piece of paper Katari had scrawled on.

"*That's* how much he wants you to deposit?"

"He said that's how much he was getting from McGinn."

"Blunt better have a mighty big couch."

Hawk smiled. "He's good for it."

Then he stopped, cocking his head and glancing skyward.

"Do you hear that?" he asked.

Alex furrowed her brow. "Hear what?"

The hum Hawk had heard grew louder, and he was sure Alex could hear it.

"That," he said, pointing toward the horizon.

A drone descended and was headed straight toward them.

"We need to get to cover now," Hawk said.

"Where are we going?" she asked.

"I saw a mosque around the corner. They should be starting their Fajr prayers soon. They wouldn't dare fire on us in a place like that."

Hawk and Alex broke into a dead sprint, racing up the docks and back toward the street. Glancing over his shoulder to catch a glimpse at how close the drone was, Hawk suddenly stopped.

"Come on, Hawk," said Alex, who continued running.

Hawk held up his hand. "No, they're not after us—not now anyway."

Alex jogged back to his side, and they both watched the drone bank hard left and head out across the water.

"Are you thinking what I'm thinking?" Alex asked.

"They're covering their tracks," Hawk said nodding.

The drone narrowed in on The Ajagar and unleashed four Hellfire missiles on the vessel. All four were direct hits. The drone peeled back east across the Arabian Sea and vanished on the horizon.

Hawk looked at the ship, which was engulfed in flames. In less than a minute, Katari's pride and joy tipped on its side and descended beneath the surface.

Alex bit her lip. "They know we're still alive."

"And I don't care," Hawk said. "Because I'm going to be coming for them."

"Who's them exactly?"

"I think I have an idea."

CHAPTER 39

Sunday
Tangier, Morocco

BLUNT AWAKENED TO THE LIGHT streaming through a small crack in his curtains. The sunrises across the Mediterranean were stunning, and most days Blunt would've fetched a complimentary cup of coffee from the lobby and enjoyed it outside on the small deck adjacent to his room. But his guest made such pleasures slightly more challenging. At the moment, Blunt cared more about getting answers out of the man than soaking up sunbeams.

Blunt was anxious to get answers, real answers. After capturing Christopher Roland's henchman, Blunt wanted to learn more about who was behind this operation. His attempts to reach Hawk and warn him had failed, likely because Hawk had gone dark, choosing to rely only on local radio transmissions to communicate with his team.

Blunt's first interrogation session with the mystery man didn't go so well. He was too loud to get anything out of him. Blunt tried several tactics to get the man to talk but to no avail. When the man began thrashing about, Blunt injected his captive with a sedative, knocking him out for several hours. When he woke up, he proceeded to do more of the same.

Not that Blunt could really blame the man either. If put in a similar situation, Blunt concluded he would likely take a similar approach. The fact that Blunt was using his hotel room to harbor an unplanned prisoner created a less than ideal situation to avoid detection, especially if Blunt wanted to maintain his low profile abroad. If he started to look suspicious, it could give the local authorities reason enough to assign a surveillance team to him.

Needing to clear his head and think, Blunt decided to inject the man with another dose of sedative to extend his long nap. After ensuring at least another few hours of peace, Blunt hung the Do Not Disturb sign on his door and lumbered upstairs to the veranda for a cup of coffee.

He was settling into his seat when his phone rang with a call from Hawk.

"Sorry I didn't call you back until now," Hawk said. "I'd already gone dark by the time you called. I wish I'd heard your message sooner."

"Apparently it didn't matter," Blunt said with a laugh. "Where's McGinn?"

"What's left of him is feeding the sharks."

"What's left of him?"

"Drone strike. Wiped out *The Ajagar*. Guess somebody in Washington didn't want to take any chances with the truth leaking out about what was going on."

"A drone strike? Unreal." He paused to take a sip of his coffee. "But why didn't they go after you? Seems rather odd, doesn't it?"

"We were running toward a more populated area before the drone changed course and zeroed in on the ship."

"Where were you when this happened? In Berbera?"

"We were near the port there, yes."

"Whoever was behind that drone strike has a helluva lot of explaining to do," Blunt said.

"We're heading back your way," Hawk said. "Can you send the plane?"

"I've been compromised, so I've got my hands full at the moment."

"Of what? A glass of scotch?"

Blunt forced a laugh. "Too early for that. No, I've captured a man, and I'm still holding him."

"You're catching about as many breaks as we are.

Got any plans for him?"

"At the moment, I'm trying to make sure this remains hush-hush. But I need to get some answers out of the guy. Any suggestions?"

"I wouldn't waste my time," Hawk said. "We know who is coming after us."

"And who's that?"

"Someone from within the CIA. Don't know any names though."

"Perhaps you're right. You and I both have plenty of enemies, even within the borders of our fine country."

"I'd like to eliminate some of them," Hawk said.

Blunt stirred his coffee for a few seconds and then placed the spoon on the saucer. "Before you do anything rash, we need to talk in person."

"So, the plane is out of the question at this point?"

"Forget the plane. Do you think you can find a way to get to the border in Djibouti?"

"I'm sure Alex and I can come up with something."

"Good. Get to the border, and then go to Camp Lemonnier. You'll find some friendly faces there. Ask for General Van Fortner."

Hawk remained silent, longer than usual.

"Hawk? You there?" Blunt asked.

"Yeah, I'm still here. Just trying to figure out if going to a U.S. military installation is a good idea at the moment."

"The CIA and the military aren't working in concert to eliminate you. If they were, it'd already have been done."

"You're not exactly instilling loads of confidence in me right now, you know that?"

Blunt chuckled. "Just figure out a way to get there, and I'll try to meet you there. My situation here is really touch-and-go, but I'll be in touch."

"Good luck," Hawk said.

"Same to you."

Blunt had been seething since he realized how he'd been double-crossed by Roland. Against better judgment, Blunt dialed Roland's number.

"I was beginning to think you weren't going to ever talk to me again," Roland said as he answered Blunt's call.

"How could you?"

"How could I do *what*?"

"Don't play coy with me," Blunt said. "We've been friends a long time. If you're at least trying to kill me, come right out and say it."

"Busted," Roland said. "I'm not going to hide it any longer since I've got a man there to do the job right now."

Blunt grew enraged. He got up out of his chair, slapped down some money on the table, and headed back to his room. As he walked down the hall, Blunt grew even angrier.

"I'll call you back in a minute," Blunt said.

He marched into his room and locked the door behind him. He peered over the balcony, estimating that the fall onto the cobblestone street below would kill the man.

Blunt worked furiously, untying the man's bindings. But the man didn't wake up. Dragging the man's body over to the porch, Blunt decided to go with the suicide route. He heaved the spy over the edge and waited inside until he heard the thud.

Once the man hit the ground, Blunt walked downstairs and out onto the street. The commotion over a dead body in the open wasn't nearly what Blunt thought it would be. Only one man knelt next to the body, while several others took pictures with their cell phones. Blunt joined them, snapping a few pictures of his own before texting the photo of the dead agent to Roland.

"You just signed your death warrant," Roland texted Blunt.

"Looks like I'd already done that but welcome to the club … and take a number," Blunt fired back.

He put his phone in his pocket and disappeared into the crowd milling around the market.

CHAPTER 40

Somaliland, Somalia

HAWK WASN'T EXCITED about the prospect of traversing Somalia's dangerous roads to get to Camp Lemonnier outside of Djibouti. Aside from the ever-challenging task of negotiating a border crossing in eastern Africa, Hawk needed transportation and cash. Those two items were vital to survival under normal circumstances. But killing several operatives from the region's prevailing terrorist organization made their situation anything but normal.

"What's our next move?" Alex asked.

"Blunt wants us to meet him at Camp Lemonnier."

"So, no plane?"

Hawk shook his head.

"Then we need to get out of here," Alex said. "It's only a matter of time before Al-Shabaab sends some men back here to investigate why their men are missing."

"And Al Hasib, too."

Alex turned to watch *The Ajagar,* which continued burning in the channel.

"Before we go though, we have to do something first."

"And what's that?"

"We need to dispose of all the Sarin and burn that plant to the ground."

Alex cocked her head to one side. "Are you sure that's a good idea? How are we going to get rid of it without endangering anyone?"

"We're going to dump it into the harbor."

"You're just going to put all the chemicals into the water?"

"Better than letting someone vaporize it and kill thousands of innocent people. Now, let's get going."

Hawk and Alex returned to Garaar's makeshift chemical plant. Garaar's body was still lying in a pool of blood when they re-entered the main lab. Hawk wasted no time in identifying the two fifty-five-gallon drums that Garaar was saving for Al Hasib.

"You think that's it?" Alex asked, gesturing toward the drums.

"While you have to consider the source, McGinn told me there were two other barrels. Not sure what purpose it would serve lying to me about that, especially if he planned to kill me."

"I'll make one more pass through the building and see what I can find."

Hawk loaded the barrels one by one onto a dolly and carted them down to the dock. He carefully cut a hole in the top of each drum before dumping them into the water.

When he returned to the building, Alex had a wide grin plastered across her face along with her computer bag slung across her shoulder.

"What is it? Did you find another barrel?" Hawk asked.

"I didn't, which is one of the reasons I'm smiling."

"And the other?"

"Two reasons. First, I got my computer back." She then held up a pair of keys. "And next, these go to Garaar's Land Rover."

"Better than McGinn's piece of junk."

The sun still hung low in the sky, but Berbera was starting to come to life. Hawk and Alex hustled over to Garaar's vehicle and fired it up.

Once they reached the compound, they found five-thousand dollars stashed in a hollow bottomed drawer in McGinn's desk.

"This ought to be enough," Hawk said.

He grabbed a scarf on the back of McGinn's chair and handed it to Alex. "You're going to need this too. We're already going to stand out. No use in making it more obvious."

Hawk also wrapped a keffiyeh around his head he found lying around before exiting the compound.

"Ready to navigate?" he asked after they climbed into the truck.

Road Number 1 was a flat highway that connected small cities throughout the country's sparsely populated northern region. Hawk expressed his displeasure at Somalian infrastructure in no uncertain terms upon studying the road map Alex pulled up on her computer.

"Who doesn't build a road along the coast? This makes no sense," he said.

"I doubt people around here are interested in making scenic drives through coastal towns."

"You have a point, though it'd be nice to slice six hours off this trip by going more direct."

"This bad boy does have four-wheel drive and tires built for desert terrain."

Hawk shook his head. "Dying of thirst in the desert is a personal nightmare of mine. I'll pass."

"Getting shot in the head is mine."

Hawk huffed a laugh through his nose. "Looks like we both got into the wrong business."

Hawk studied the map once more before hitting the road. Road Number 1 went west out of Berbera and continued for a long stretch until it headed north. It eventually turned back east and wound up at the border of Djibouti.

***

THE FIRST NINE HOURS of their ten-hour trip to the border was rather uneventful until they approached Saylac, a coastal border town located about sixty kilometers south of Djibouti. Suspicious if the detour was real, Hawk complied with the uniformed man directing him to take a dirt road due west.

After two minutes of driving down a winding road, Hawk noticed there wasn't anyone else around. They zipped through a neighborhood, but it appeared abandoned.

"I don't like this at all," Hawk said. "I'm turning around."

Hawk hit the brakes and backed up into an alleyway. But he didn't get very far when Alex screamed.

"Hawk! Look out!"

A black SUV rolled up behind them, and two men brandishing rifles were in the process of shimmying out the backseat windows, presumably to begin firing. Hawk shoved the gear back into drive and hit the gas. The kicked up dust gave Hawk a momentary advantage, creating a smokescreen to disappear into. But it also created an inescapable trail.

Bullets riddled the back of their vehicle as gunfire erupted.

"Think you can find me a way out of this mess?" Hawk asked.

Alex typed away on her computer. "It's so much easier to help you when I'm not being shot at."

"Just find me a damn road—no, forget it. I've got an idea."

Hawk swung the car around, spinning one hundred eighty degrees, which caught his assailants off guard. He remembered seeing a large dirt mound about two hundred meters before the SUV roared up behind them. His plan was simple: use the dusty trail to his advantage.

Hawk roared back down the road toward the mound.

"You might want to put that thing away and hold on," Hawk said to Alex.

She shoved the computer back into her bag and tucked it beneath her feet.

Then Hawk slowed down.

"What are you doing?" she asked.

"Saving our lives."

The SUV was right behind them now and firing

more bullets. The back windshield finally shattered, and several bullets whizzed toward the front seat and hit the windshield.

"I'd like to know some specifics please," Alex said as she stared at the mound in front of them. "This doesn't seem to be—"

Hawk jerked the wheel, flinging an unprepared Alex to the left. He'd maneuvered the SUV out of the way just in time to see the SUV behind them go careening up the mound and over. The assailants' vehicle landed hard on its side. Hawk then slowed down and took aim for the roof.

"You're going to get us killed," Alex said.

"If we don't kill them first, they're definitely going to kill us."

Hawk jammed his foot on the gas and barreled straight for the vehicle. The aftermath was a mangled pile of metal wrapped around the front of their truck.

Wasting no time, Hawk jumped out and crept toward the other side of the SUV. He climbed on top and shot each one of the men in the head, except the driver, who was trying to say something.

"What was that?" Hawk asked.

The driver's face was a bloodied mess.

"Others will come for you," the man said. "We know what you did in Berbera."

"Maybe they'll stop after they see what I did to

you," Hawk said before shooting the man twice in the head and once in the chest.

Hawk rushed back toward his vehicle when he noticed Alex standing on the other side, her bag slung over her shoulder.

"Good going, Hawk. Our ride is about to go up in flames," she said pointing to the smoke pouring out the rear of the vehicle.

She took off running in an effort to escape the imminent explosion. Hawk was right behind her.

"Maybe next time you can think of a plan that's not so destructive. Getting the job done at all costs isn't always the smartest move."

"Are you worried about how we're going to get to the border?"

"Alive and in one piece? Yeah—I am."

"Well, don't worry. You still got that five grand?"

"Thinking about getting a taxi?"

Hawk shook his head. "It'd be too easy for some other Al-Shabaab thugs to find us before we get there. We need to travel a little more discreetly."

***

AN HOUR LATER, Hawk and Alex were saddled on a pair of camels that set them back three-thousand dollars. It was more than market price, but Hawk didn't have time to bicker over the price. Alex managed to talk the man into throwing in some traditional attire for her and Hawk to wear. Two hours later, they were approaching the Djibouti border.

"This ought to be interesting," Alex said. "I want to hear how you're going to explain that we arrived in the country via plane but now we're exiting on camels."

Hawk grinned. "I'm going to let you explain that one. You're the one who speaks French, not me. Besides, I bet they'll let us do anything we want once we gift them these camels."

"Untraceable bribes are the best kind," Alex said.

"Not that it matters out here."

It took Alex less than fifteen minutes to explain to the border patrol agent what they were doing on camels. He told them he couldn't permit them to leave, not without the authority of a higher-ranking government officer. Then Alex turned on her charm. She asked the man if that was necessary if she was going to give him their camels.

Out came the stamp—and they were through into Djibouti.

Hawk offered five-hundred dollars to another agent on the other side to drive them to Camp Lemonnier. Once there, they asked for the gate MP to contact General Van Fortner and that they needed to speak to him on the orders of J.D. Blunt. After a few phone calls and verification of their identities,

Hawk and Alex were forced to surrender their weapons and were taken via an armed escort to a hangar to meet General Fortner.

Fortner emerged from an office door in the hangar to greet his guests. While Blunt had mentioned that Fortner was twenty years his younger, Hawk struggled to see it. Perhaps it was the effects of leading a military installation located in one of the hottest regions on the planet. Or maybe it was just life in the military. Whatever the reason, Fortner's face was leathery, his hat covering up what wisps of hair escaped. Hawk noted that he'd never seen any fresh-faced generals, even ones that made the rank far ahead of their peers, even ones that didn't live in such harsh environments.

Fortner broke into a smile and offered his hand to Hawk and Alex.

"You must be Brady Hawk," Fortner said, shaking Hawk's hand. He turned toward Alex. "And you're Alex Duncan?"

They both nodded.

"It's my pleasure to meet both of you. J.D. spoke highly of you both the last time we talked."

"When was that?" Hawk asked.

"Several weeks ago when he was trying to escape that shit storm Washington was raining down on him."

"I'm glad someone has his back."

"That's a dwindling crowd these days."

"We know that all too well," Alex said.

Fortner looked Hawk and Alex up and down. It hadn't even occurred to Hawk how questionable their grimy clothes might appear to someone else.

"Rough trip over here?" Fortner said with a grin.

"If you only knew the half of it," Hawk said.

"Let me guess—terrorists, guns, camels, desert? Does that about cover it?"

"How'd you know?" Alex asked.

Fortner shook his head. "I live in Djibouti on the border of Somalia. That's called Monday around here."

"Think you can get us to Tuesday?" Hawk asked.

"Tell me what you need, and I'll make it happen."

Hawk's phone buzzed. "Excuse me, General. I need to take this call."

Hawk stepped away from the crowd and left Alex to charm the general. He glanced down at his phone before answering it.

"Now's not a good time, Emily," Hawk said in a whisper.

"I need your help."

"I'm not sure I can help you right now," he said.

"Please, I'm begging you. They're going to kill me if you don't do what Parker asks you to do. I need you to come to Cape Town."

CHAPTER 41

Cape Town, South Africa

EMILY THORNTON WAS all too aware that she'd lost a good man in Brady Hawk. It was a steep price to pay but a necessary one for someone who feels committed to the cause. Yet the cause had lost its fervor, though not its importance. Managing the surging number of shadowy black ops organizations had been reduced to an endless game of whack-a-mole. To ignore these groups would lead to a world overrun with tyrant leaders. But to snuff them out had grown exhausting and dangerous. There were fewer resources to deal with the burgeoning problem that had spread like a cancer across the globe.

At the center of all these groups was the one Emily wanted to see taken down more than anything. It was why she stayed with Searchlight even as she acknowledged that the organization's tactics often rode roughshod over legal lines. However, Emily's latest assignment had her straddling the fence between succeeding in her mission and maintaining a shred of authenticity in her relationship with Hawk. Their romance had been real years ago when they were working together in Jordan with the Peace Corps, despite the fact that it was first part of a covert op. Hawk, her secondary assignment, was born out of opportunism. A chance to lure an elite-trained Navy Seal to work for them couldn't be ignored. It's all she ever mentioned to Hawk. She never wanted to tell him the primary reason she was there. The assignment was too dark and too evil. She knew he'd never look at her the same way again if he ever found out.

Yet here she was years later faced with a quandary that pitted duty and devoted obsession against the only man she'd ever loved. To move forward, she resigned herself to the fact that Hawk was a lost cause for her. Emily figured there weren't enough days left in their lives to rebuild the trust that they'd once had. It was over—and it made what she was about to do that much easier.

Hawk just might try to kill me once he realizes we want to use Alex for bait, but there's no other way.

Emily had perfected the art of manipulation and was prepared to use it when the situation called for it. If there was ever a time when she needed to do so, this was the moment. The guilt Emily felt over lying to Hawk about her supposedly being in danger from Searchlight would easily be assuaged after she took down the person at the center of The Chamber. Once The Chamber was weakened, a domino effect would ensue as the other players vied to assume the role as top dog. But no other group was positioned as strategically as The Chamber, and neither was one resourced as well either. Weapons and money were one thing, but The Chamber also possessed a stable of highly-trained operatives who could remove any world leader from power if its decision makers so desired. Destroying The Chamber would make the world a safer place, that much Emily believed. And she held this belief as if it was religious dogma.

Her phone buzzed, and she answered the call from Kade Parker.

"Did you have any luck with Hawk?" he asked.

Emily sighed. "He said he'd do it."

"Excellent. I knew he'd come around. What'd you do? Turn on your Thornton charm?"

She ignored his question. "For the record, I'm not happy about this. You better succeed or else we might become Hawk's next target."

"Oh, once we get what we need out of him, he will become target zero on our hit list," he said. "Perhaps I'll even give you the honors."

"That's one I'll take a pass on."

"Suit yourself. Good work, Agent Thornton. Once you get confirmation that Hawk and Alex are on the plane headed to see you, I'll send you the rest of the details about how to proceed."

Emily hung up. Hawk had promised her no such thing, but she was confident that he'd cave and come to her rescue.

CHAPTER 42

Camp Lemonnier
Djibouti City, Djibouti

HAWK LOOKED AT ALEX still engaged in conversation with General Fortner while calling Blunt to find out where he was. It'd been hours since they'd spoken, and there was no sign of Blunt. When he finally answered Hawk's call, a conversation occurred that rattled Hawk to his core.

"Are you going to be joining us soon?" Hawk asked. "We've made it to Camp Lemonnier."

"So I hear," Blunt said. "General Fortner gave me a call to vet you."

"Good to know he's being careful."

"You can never be too cautious in this day and age. You know that as well as anybody."

"Are you in route?"

"Not yet," Blunt said. "I'm afraid something else has come up that I need to take care of."

"Do you have another assignment for us? And preferably one that doesn't involve working with a backstabbing traitor."

Blunt waited a few seconds before answering. "I wouldn't recommend overstaying your welcome. It seems you've made some enemies at the CIA or at least some division of it, and who knows how long before they convince one of the military personnel there to take you out. What better place to do it than one where you feel safe all the time?"

"I never feel safe any more."

"Good. That's what'll keep you alive."

Hawk took a deep breath, unsure of how to broach the next subject.

"I spoke with Emily Thornton," he said.

"And you're still alive?" Blunt fired back.

"Why would you—?"

"Look, Hawk, it's dangerous times out there, and you need to be careful. She's working with Searchlight and could pose a serious threat to you *and* Alex."

"Why Alex? I mean, Emily wants me to bring her with me and—"

"Where? Why? What is this all about?"

"She needs my help, Senator. Searchlight is after her now."

"That's bullshit. She's one of their top operatives. Go if you don't believe me, but don't take Alex with you."

"Why not? Alex and I work great together as a team. I feel much better about my chances of saving Emily with Alex on the team."

"Listen to me, Hawk. Emily's life isn't in danger. She wants you down there because they want to use Alex."

"Use Alex? Like as a hacker?"

"No. It's for something far worse, I'm afraid."

Hawk turned his back to Alex and General Fortner, gazing at the choppy waters in the distance. "You think they're going to hurt her?"

"It doesn't matter because they don't care if she gets hurt or not."

"Then why on earth would they need her?" Hawk asked.

"To use her as bait."

"Bait?"

"You heard me: bait." Blunt paused to let the gravity of his statement sink in.

"Who could she possibly be used as bait for? She's a loner. She has hardly any friends and—"

"Her mother. They want to use her as bait for her mother."

"Her mother? But her mother's—"

"Dead?" Blunt said. "No, not hardly. The woman Alex knows as Kathryn Duncan, the woman that gave birth to Alex and reportedly died in an accident on the

Beltway—she's actually Katarina Petrov. And the CIA has been trying to capture her for years. They even had the same plan to use Alex as bait at one point before she went all white knight and blew the whistle on some of their covert operations that weren't exactly operating within the confines of the law."

"Would Alex be in danger?"

"From what I know of Katarina Petrov, she wouldn't hesitate to kill her own daughter. I always thought it was a foolish plan, but the CIA was adamant that it would work."

"And you hired Alex to keep her safe?"

"Exactly. That's why I never wanted her in the field. It had the potential to jeopardize her and compromise a mission, especially toy with your better judgment."

"So why does everyone want to kill Katarina Petrov so badly?"

"She's the head of The Chamber."

"*The* Chamber? The one you used to work for?"

"That's the one," Blunt said.

"And you're just now getting around to telling me this? Don't you think that's kind of important? All my missions could be at risk because of Alex."

"Hard to stuff that genie back into the bottle, especially when you can't talk to her about it."

"You're sure she doesn't know?" Hawk asked, incredulous.

"Not a clue, and let's keep it that way. You just keep her safe, understand?"

Blunt kept talking without waiting for an answer, but Hawk was lost in his own world. He watched a plane touch down on the runway in front of him, the blast from the roaring jet engines making it impossible for Hawk to hear anything Blunt was saying.

"What was that?" Hawk said loudly.

"Oh, never mind."

"Just to be clear—you don't want us to go to Cape Town then?" Hawk asked.

"Under no circumstances," Blunt said. "You stay put until I call you."

"Roger that," Hawk said. "Be safe."

Hawk hung up the phone and resisted the urge to turn back around and look at Alex. He wanted to catch that secret glimpse of her, a beautiful woman whose personality and looks had grown on him quickly, more quickly than any other woman he'd known.

Stop it, Hawk. Keep your focus. This is about making the world a safer place, not hooking up with a beautiful woman.

Hawk spun around on his heel and walked back toward the conversation he'd been conspicuously absent from for the past ten minutes.

"Is everything all right?" Alex asked.

Hawk nodded. "Everything is good, but we need

to get moving."

"Without Blunt?" she said, her brow furrowed.

"Yes, we've got business to attend to elsewhere," Hawk said, looking General Fortner in the eyes. "He was wondering if you might be able to arrange transportation for us, General."

"And where are you two jet setters off to next?" Fortner asked.

"We're going to Cape Town."

THE END

ACKNOWLEDGMENTS

I am grateful to so many people who have helped with the creation of this project and the entire Brady Hawk series. Morocco is one of my favorite places I've ever visited and loved setting some scenes in the book there.

Krystal Wade has been a fantastic help in handling the editing of this book, and Dwight Kuhlman has produced another great audio version for your listening pleasure.

I would also like to thank my advance reader team for all their input in improving this book along with all the other readers who have enthusiastically embraced the story of Brady Hawk. Stay tuned ... there's more Brady Hawk coming soon.

ABOUT THE AUTHOR

R.J. PATTERSON is an award-winning writer living in southeastern Idaho. He first began his illustrious writing career as a sports journalist, recording his exploits on the soccer fields in England as a young boy. Then when his father told him that people would pay him to watch sports if he would write about what he saw, he went all in. He landed his first writing job at age 15 as a sports writer for a daily newspaper in Orangeburg, S.C. He later attended earned a degree in newspaper journalism from the University of Georgia, where he took a job covering high school sports for the award-winning *Athens Banner-Herald* and *Daily News*.

He later became the sports editor of *The Valdosta Daily Times* before working in the magazine world as an editor and freelance journalist. He has won numerous writing awards, including a national award for his investigative reporting on a sordid tale surrounding an NCAA investigation over the University of Georgia football program.

R.J. enjoys the great outdoors of the Northwest while living there with his wife and three children. He still follows sports closely. He also loves connecting with readers and would love to hear from you. To stay updated about future projects, connect with him over Facebook or on the inter-webs at www.RJPbooks.com and sign up for his newsletter to get deals and updates.

Made in the USA
Middletown, DE
03 April 2018